Coda

Thea Astley is Australia's most important contemporary writer.

Thea Astley was born in Brisbane and studied at the University of Queensland. Since 1958 she has published twelve novels, winning the Miles Franklin Award three times: in 1962 for *The Well Dressed Explorer*, in 1965 for *The Slow Natives* (which also won the Moomba Award), and in 1972 for *The Acolyte*; and winning The *Age* Book of the Year Award for *A Kindness Cup*. Her collection of short stories, *Hunting the Wild Pineapple*, won the Townsville Literary Foundation Award in 1979, her novel *Beachmasters* won the Australian Literature Society Gold Medal in 1987, and *It's Raining in Mango* won the Steele Rudd Award and the 1988 FAW ANA Literature Award. In 1990 *Reaching Tin River* won the New South Wales Award for fiction. Her last book was *Vanishing Points*.

Thea Astley now writes full-time from her home in the hills in the New South Wales south coast.

Also by Thea Astley

Coda

THEA ASTLEY

MINERVA

First published 1993 by William Heinemann Australia
Published 1994 by Minerva
a part of Reed Books Australia
22 Salmon Street, Port Melbourne, Victoria 3207
a division of Reed International Books Australia Pty Limited

Typeset in Garamond No. 3 by Bookset Pty. Ltd.
Printed and bound in Australia by Australian Print Group

National Library of Australia
    cataloguing-in-publication data:

Astley, Thea, 1925– .
    Coda.

    ISBN 1 86330 392 8.

    I. Title.

A823.3

Part One

A representative for an electronics firm travelling between Condamine and Cunnamulla last Monday noticed an elderly couple sitting beside the highway midway between Moonie and St George, apparently having a picnic lunch. On his return two days later, he observed the same couple still seated beside their spread rug. He stopped his car to ask if he could be of assistance as they appeared to have no means of transport.

Our good Samaritan, Mr Bob Trugrove of Condamine Electronics, managed to get both of them into his car, whereupon he drove them immediately to hospital.

The couple, he reported later to police in Condamine, were extremely old and did not seem to understand what he said to them. They were obviously distressed. Their water flask was empty and the only food remaining was a small packet of crackers.

There was evidence, too, of distress of a personal nature and their clothes were soiled and in need of changing. The woman insisted they were waiting for the return of their son-in-law. Inquiries are under way.

Police state that there has been an alarming increase in so-called 'granny dumping' throughout the country.

Condamine Examiner, *16 January 1992*

I'M LOSING MY NOUNS, she admitted.

God knows she was losing other things as well. Hearing. Sight. Tenses. Moods. A grammarian's funeral! But the nouns worried her most, proper nouns especially—names of people and places. Proper and common. Oh yes, it was not all there. And it was those nouns from the present tense or the past perfect—yes, that!—she'd lost grips with. Try her out on a preterite or a pluperfect of forty, fifty years ago

5

and everything flowed like syrup, filling each crevice of memory.

A funny thing about all this: she was starting to think of herself in the third person when she went back to where the nouns and the verbs all stayed in place in the sweetest logical sequence, as if she were some other. Which she was, the body replenishing its cell structure every seven years.

Was that me?

The wrapping's changed!

The me of me rattles on, nounless.

It had been a bad few months.

You know, Tolstoy was wrong with that little aphorism he tossed off in the Austen manner about families: All unhappy families *are* the same in their wretchedness. There are no grading lines in *un*-happiness. Most, as far as she could see or remember, simply blundered about in a kind of economic fog, groping the walls of their caves with daylight-seeking palms. Lucky if they landed on a bit of bat dung.

'When you want to stop moving,' Daisy had said, 'you're dead.'

Those were prognostic words.

Daisy was her friend. She was all wrinkles with brooches everywhere. For four — was it five? — years, they used to meet at a bus stop near the town hall to do the caffs in the big stores and have a nose around. What a survivor! *Hot diggety, Daisy!* 'I've got me shack,' she used to say, 'and me radio and me telly.' (Ruining her possessive adjectives!) 'I've got everything I need. Can't need much more at seventy-eight, can I?'

She had her nouns, too, those days, proper and common. Could run through a list of recalled people, places and objects, no sweat, never missing a beat. *Daisy, I miss you.*

She was the link, the tie, the anchorage of flat-voiced comfort over endless cups of tea.

There's more to this story, she said to her. *It will be pointillist. A spot here. A dab there. As it comes. Hang in there!*

But she wanted to stop moving. She'd had the moving. She longed for the slack of the wind.

That's Shamrock and Brain, Kathleen remembered, pausing in the town mall, humping her bag between the schoolkids taking the morning off and bargain hunters at the summer sales. Her thoughts were angular, sharpened to that horrible moment of wounded antagonism where she could wipe her hands free of both. Unwanted and unwanting. No, that wasn't strictly true. She found herself shaking her head, unsure of anything except that she was there and on her own. 'Face it, lady,' she said aloud. 'This is it.'

She could afford a cuppa as the morning heat swelled, needed a cuppa, needed time to think of Shamrock obliterated in her own fizzle of spit and howl, of recriminations puling across the grievances of decades.

'It's impossible, Mum,' her daughter had told her. 'Can't you see that? You can't go on living there, not the way you are now, forgetting every damn thing. And there's no way you can possibly fit in at our place. Apart from the smallness.'

Is it small? Kathleen had asked, looking at what seemed acres of tile and wall-to-wall. *Is it?*

Shamrock had crimped her mouth into refusals and after a long pause had said, 'Well, it's too late now. It's all arranged. There's this retirement place. Come and see it. Just see, for God's sake. You know it's better. You can't always depend on neighbours. If you'd only try to remember and not wander off the way you've been doing lately. I can't cope with that. None of us can. You have to try to remember.'

Up north in this steaming no-count town

where she had been born, grown up and lived so long ago now, there had been too much to remember, drunk with youth, especially in those years of early marriage, seeking the idyll yet somehow missing it. Solitariness, despite people, shops, work-mates, friends. Inexplicable. Solitariness nibbling away even in the middle of parties, dances, pillow-talk. Her parents had moved south when the war ended but were killed within the year by a vigorous semitrailer insisting on its right of way, and Daisy had become a scrawled signature on infrequent letters from Melbourne.

Although she had Ronald and later the children, she was involved in clutter at the store through red-rimmed evenings wrestling the accounts into shape, chasing overdue and often never-paid bills. At night, lying sleepless in the scratch of weather, she wondered about the meridian of marriage, the peak point from where everything began its descent into the chafe of ordinariness.

She might have asked the frizzy waitress this, did ask, *When is the meridian of marriage?* to a sideways look that dragged her into now.

How long had she been squatting at this plastic table under the fig tree in the mall? Her elbow had stopped bleeding but there were rusty stains on the front of her skirt. She licked a finger and rubbed at them absent-mindedly. Mugged in Brisbane, she decided. Patched and peeled in Townsville.

Coffee, she recalled suddenly. And milk. A twitch of skirt vanished with her demand for what had become a communion ichor.

The pecking order. Life was dominated by a pecking order in town, suburb, home, an order against which everyone fought: she and the waitress, she and Ronald, she and the kids.

Remembering.

Then.

There had been all the stage props of a low-rent production of *South Pacific*: rattling palms, sagging shacks eaten out by woodworm and salt, a sharp wind combing the water onto the cooling sand as the sky darkened, and the endless biting of midges where they huddled by a fire under the rocks of the headland. The last ferry was lurching across Cleveland Bay to the island.

'Miss it,' he had pleaded, his face young and unsure in the dark-light dark-light of the jumping flames. His ill-fitting khakis hung like

sacking. She was aware how thin his wrists were
as he reached over to stoke the fire with pieces
of driftwood that sputtered blue.

'No,' she had said and saw the word bite
into his mouth. 'No. I've got to get to work in
the morning.' The bones of his working hands
stuck innocently out, sharpened by firelight.

'Please.' He looked across at her and then
at the riding light of the drunken boat as it
rocked across water. 'Don't make me plead.
Please.'

She didn't intend to be brutal but she
found herself saying, 'It's time we doused this,'
and began throwing handfuls of sand onto the
fire. 'I can't. I simply can't.'

They had met a fortnight before on the
island five miles across the water. She and Daisy
had gone across for the weekend and after dinner had wandered into the cavernous lounge
room of the pub where a small group of soldiers, time-filling before they were demobbed,
were taking their leave in this down-home version of island hells they had left to the north.
Daisy urged her and within minutes she was
sitting at the out-of-tune upright angled across
one corner of the room, while the soldiers clustered around as she banged out sentimental
wartime ballads. Wind and palm-rattle came in
vertical slices through the wooden louvres that

11

•

Coda

acted as walls, and the young men's voices strained seawards while outside the sea gabbled answers as it nuzzled the beach, its watery descant dragged by an egg-frail moon. Fireflies sparked messages.

Did *she*? Had *she*?

Even later that evening she found herself strolling with this young man along a windy beach, moving away from the pub and stumbling up the rocky knoblands of the front until they were turned back by a coast-watcher.

'The war's over, anyway,' the young man had argued with the over-zealous fellow.

'Orders,' the coastguard said, straining to catch their features in his torch, 'until the treaty's finally signed. You're lucky, mate. You've missed out on Wewak.'

'I'm coming back, not going.'

His thin face was earnest under its ochre patina from Atebrin, and he gripped Kathleen's arm so fiercely she felt his fingers digging at bone.

'Well, you'll be demobbed soon, mate.'

'And I can't wait,' he said bitterly. 'King and country! Shit!'

'Now, now,' the coastguard said. 'That's not nice.'

Kathleen saw the tense profile beside her sketched briefly in torchlight, the eye a straining blue.

'Oh shut up!' she had said suddenly. 'Just shut up!' The fingers on her arm squeezed their thanks.

They didn't miss the ferry that weekend. When she returned a week later, hoping that he too might have managed leave from the army barracks outside the town, the reunion, the recognition of something shared, established a harmony deeper than either believed in, if either had thought about it. They hiked through the scrub away from the old hotel and the jetty, climbing down the granite boulders of Rocky Bay. Isolation was complete. Gulls screamed across the dipping waves that were so clean in their shocking blue, there might be no memory of flesh mangle and stink of the dying and already dead on those other lyric islands. They swam in the rubbery tide of the inlet, splashing like kids, to stagger back to the beach-line gasping and spluttering with draughts of sea.

'I could stay here for ever,' he had said, lying back on the whitest and most burning of sand, remembering the Solomons and Tulagi and his father's store. Nothing left now, he had told her, after the civilians had been evacuated before the raids that had destroyed everything his father had built up. 'For ever.' He lingered over the repeated words that were part of another dream.

She was more of a realist.

'You couldn't. Only for a little while. You'd get bored.'

He jerked up, swinging round to face her, jamming his fingers deeply into the shell grit so that they vanished to the knuckles. 'You don't know about islands, do you? You don't understand. How could you?'

She repeated stubbornly, 'Everyone gets fed up, needs change. You'd get bored, I tell you.'

He was silent so long she began to suspect sulks, but he was looking at her so intently she found herself turning away, watching her toes as she dug them in and out, in and out of the shingle.

At last he asked, 'Is that a prompt? Should I say not with you? Never bored with you?'

'Oh no!' she had cried. 'Oh no! It wasn't intended.'

Embarrassed, she began tracing doubtful lines in the sand, erasing then tracing again. She scribbled arabesques of nothing and the sea scrawled its own messages of shell and kelp on the tide edge.

He had been idiotically rash, she realised now, fifty years on.

'Let's give it a try,' he said, only half joking. 'How about it?'

Everyone was doing foolish things those years, racing impulsively to ruin.

'How about what?' As if she hadn't known! As if!

'Us. My heart aches,' he said and touched his groin with simple candour.

Us. We. Us. We. Us. We.

Uswe.

It was as simple as that.

Although there were patterns in the past, she conceded, relationships had blurred and now there were only these brilliant sharp-edged pictures smashing against memory, bringing surf-whack aches.

Before Ronald? Had there been a before?

There had been encounters, some momentary, some promising definition and a hope of endurance. They belonged to some other life, not hers. Sweltering in the mall, her third coffee steaming at her elbow, there sprang onto the mind-screen, uncalled, a curly office relief clerk who played drums, a sombre traveller in electrical goods, a too good-looking airforce officer who flew out before she could fly in, and the almost forgotten face of a merchant skipper on a British cargo ship that had resumed trading in the last month of the Pacific war. (Down by the breakwater on the turgid river came the long-drawn wail of a boat.)

'Background music,' she said aloud.

How had they met? she asked herself, wrestling with memory.

She had stepped accidentally into his hotel room and briefly into his mind, in Sydney where she had gone for a holiday with an older girl from the typing pool. 'Daisy?' she had asked the thickening air.

The door, which was opened fully onto the darkness beyond, offered no sense of welcome but suggested all the hollowness of an empty theatre (the cast late, the technicians on strike, the audience turned away). Behind, the corridor stretched, an empty laneway of hard yellow.

Outlined by reflected glow from buildings across George Street, a bulkiness by the window stirred and loomed. A lamp was switched on. Involuntarily she stepped back a pace from this huge fellow, a bland round-faced towerer with a built-in curve to the mouth, almost but not quite clown-like, giving the impression of continuing mirth.

'As you can see,' he said, 'no.'

Despite his amusement she had continued standing puzzled in the doorway, embarrassed by her night attire, fingers pleating her dressing-gown tie.

But this was her room, she explained. They had arranged to meet.

He dropped his past tense like a stone, Kathleen remembered. 'Was.' The flat thud of the syllable hit her arrested feet. 'I believe she has been elevated, moved up a floor. Promoted to the bridge.'

He was a man who dealt in final decisions, she could tell.

The shot-blue silk of his smoking jacket, its almost ecclesiastical bravura, overwhelmed her. He was brimming with liquor and loneliness. From the next room came the sound of a radio, Satchelmouth drooling through 'A Kiss to Build a Dream on', a chocolate flow that permeated the air of this drab upstairs stage.

'I'm terribly sorry,' she remembered saying, foxed by the inanity of words.

'Not at all.' Infinitesimally the bulk of him appeared to move closer. 'Not — at — all.' He laughed, an abrupt bark of a laugh, and said, 'Do stay. All very proper. Do have a small drink with me in this God-forsaken town. I can offer Scotch . . .' he began an untidy rummaging in a drawer '. . . or Scotch. Not terribly exciting, I'm afraid.'

What had possessed her then? What? She knew no one in Sydney but Daisy, who had vanished that morning in a flurry of jumpers and scarves to visit old friends in the Blue

Mountains, and her own loneliness was underscored inexplicably by the man and the room and the music so that she said, encouraged by the light of the place and the door open behind her, 'Why not?' Sophisticated, she thought. Poised, she thought.

Moving lightly, he pulled out the other chair for her with a desperate florid courtesy, uttering his name. She could not remember it now, sitting in the mall. Benedict? she wondered. Bernard? Yet she told him hers and he repeated the 'Kathleen' and asked 'Irish?', without waiting for an answer.

She held the drink he had poured into a tooth mug and they sat looking at each other in the abominable awkwardness of a failed party.

'Well,' he said, regarding her curiously over the rim of his own glass. 'Well.'

Unexpectedly her own laughter was caught in cough and wheeze with the first sip. God, she could still remember the coughing, the fear she would choke in this stranger's room. But he had helped her recovery with the most tentative of back slaps and somehow, some gauche how, she found herself rattling on as if he had freed words as well, talking of herself, the north. She could barely recall his replies now but she knew he had admitted to being master of a cargo vessel plying between London, the far East and

Australia. He came from Suffolk, he told her, and round about his third drink (taken with a desperate compulsion) confessed, an ironic twist to the mouth, to being a bachelor.

Common ground, something to marvel at, the world's smallness, came when she dredged up the name of his ship from a recently typed invoice and lading consignment. Daisy, her friend Daisy, she had been anxious to explain, and she both worked for the same shipping company, nothing exciting, simply clerical work, beating typewriters to death.

This small and innocuous moment of union was suddenly ripped apart by her returned buddy, stuffed with drama and accompanied by the hotel manager fearful of scandal. There had been voluble explanations, cries of protest, everything a shamefaced blur.

Yet the next evening she allowed him to take her to a show at the old Tivoli. She had never seen vaudeville before and found the crudity of the acts appalling from the moment the curtain rose. It was during a scene where some check-pantsed ocker kept groping suggestively in a bubble bath filled with a naked blonde and an evasive soap cube that she found laughter stopped dead in her throat like a plug. She turned to her companion and saw that he was hugely amused. 'Not funny,' she couldn't refrain from whispering. 'Not funny at all.' She winced with her discomfort and he allowed her to suffer only a few more minutes.

'I think we've had enough of this,' he suggested kindly. In the neon glare of George Street he seemed filled with contrition. 'Sailors are crude animals.'

After she returned north, beautifully typed and mis-spelled letters arrived at her workplace from ports along the eastern seaboard. 'Hello,' he wrote. 'I keep saying hello to my chief officer. I think I caught it from you. When may I say hello in person? I have discussed this with him and his advice is to proceed.'

Should I? she had asked Daisy, who had only giggled and said *well, any storm in a port!*

They met at Queens Hotel on the waterfront. She remembered his letters better than his face.

He was drunk, lordly and staggering. Other diners were stunned by his ducal assumptions as he ushered her to a table.

'I have thought of you for three weeks,' he confessed. 'I have thought all that time between saying hello and getting drunk.'

She hardly knew what to say to that. His voice seemed over-loud and diners were regarding them with interest.

'I know I'm far too old for this sort of hi-jinks.' He belched and apologised with inebriated formality. 'I know I'm a thousand years older than you. But would you consider marrying me?'

The food had not even arrived. She was mesmerised by the craziness of his proposition, idiotically tempted by thoughts of escape from the job, the heat, the town.

'But I don't even know you.'

His voice rose as he brushed objections away with drunken hands. 'No one knows anybody. Absolutely no one. In fact the only one I really know, *really* know . . .' He stopped as if he had forgotten already '. . . is the old girl. My ship. She's the only one I know. After this meal, if it ever comes, I'll take you to say hello to her. You'll love her.'

After that they ate almost in silence. The other diners stopped watching and occasionally, but only occasionally, she found his fogged eyes regarding her.

Perhaps he was invigorated by the tropic air, for his step became lighter as they walked to the docks afterwards and he moved with the eagerness, she recognised now, of lover towards lover. There were lascars on night watch. There were short exchanges, friendly, she observed, and his tipsiness evaporated in direct ratio to the shortening of distance between him and the love object.

On the bridge he opened a door with

panache. The cabin was large, functional and gleaming with highly polished wood. There were leather chairs and a giant slab of a desk whose solidity her fingers involuntarily stroked while her lips, unwilled, shaped O's of approval which he observed, drunk or not. Outside and below, the docks squatted under sky-dark, listening to tides round their massive piles, yarning about the sea.

'You like it, don't you?' he said. 'I can see you like it.' The absurdity of his eagerness! 'You can travel back with me.'

She asked how. Already he was foraging for a drink.

'Here of course. Right here. Large enough for two.' He smiled as he poured himself a drink. 'No, I know you don't want one. Look, it's quite simple. As master, I do as I like. I'm free to take my wife back with me. Would you like that? Say you would. I would.'

Baffled, she shook her head, not a denial so much as an admission of puzzlement, whereupon he lumped down into the swivel chair behind the desk to hulk, sipping and watching in a fall of silence heavy as a theatre curtain dropping on the final act. Desolation settled over his shoulders, the glass of Scotch, shutting him off.

'Marry me,' he suggested again. He took another sip. 'Please marry me.'

'I still don't know you. Not even here. Less. Not . . .'

'Not what?'

'Not even with your real wife.'

'Oh God, she's a tolerant old lady. Forget that. As I say, no one knows anyone. Ever.' He hiccupped slightly.

'Let's talk about this tomorrow, hey?'

'Why tomorrow?'

'Because . . . oh look, I'm sorry to say this . . . but you'll be sober then. You'll have had a rethink.'

She edged up from the settee, uncomfortable with possibilities, while courteously, gently, he matched her movement but stood so far apart from her she wondered. Why did he never use her name? Why had he made no move to hold her hand, at least, or begin those wearying overtures of the relief clerk, the traveller in electrical goods, the too presumptuous airforce lieutenant?

'You may kiss me if you want,' she offered, putting her face up and looking for resolution, curious to see his reaction to such forwardness. There was something skewed about the whole business. Something.

Keeping good manners on tippy toes, he moved deliberately across the cabin and placed the most diffident of hands upon her upper arms, sliding them (*abeam*, he might have said) behind her shoulders until she was bracketed and though touched, clasped, felt untouched. There was no response in either of them. It was being alone with aloneness.

She could smell starch on his shirt and idly that traitor thought recurred: I could reach England this way. I could get out of this town. I could stop beating that typewriter. Ah, shame! His arms enclosed her as impersonally as a printed parenthesis and the touch of his mouth on hers held the papery brush of fleshly indifference. He knew all this too.

Raising his head he gazed down from under those sadly comic eyebrows and she understood at once.

'It's years. I haven't had a woman in years.' He was mumbling something, driven to confession perhaps, addressing a point on the cabin's far wall.

'How . . . how did you manage?'

'Boys,' he was not quite explaining. 'Boys.'

The quiver of resolved doubt. All explanation surged and then was obliterated by a fatalism she understood—well, she was sure she understood. Boys. Did that matter, did that really matter in whatever coupling they might form, each using the other ever so explicitly, if only she could be offered passage out of her present?

Of course she decided against it, but when

they met the next morning, she early, he late, sobriety and panic made him blunt.

'It's not on,' he informed without preamble. 'I can't. I was drunk. It's just not on.'

She hadn't even had time to greet him and couldn't resist asking, 'What's not?'

'Marriage. The whole thing. I simply can't. Not fair to either. No tears, please. Can't stand tears.'

'Why tears? Tears for what?'

He stared down at her through a long wry line of boys while his mouth twisted with self-disgust, or disgust for the world.

'Well, you never know. It's scenes. Can't bear bloody scenes.'

Sweating and horribly sober now in noontide, he was urging her into the dining room of the hotel to meet his luncheon guests. Their name was ominous. Captain Storm. Mrs Storm. Kathleen found she was fighting back giggles rather than tears as Captain Storm explained that there were others called Gale and Southerly. They were resoundingly jolly, and she suspected that the two beautifully clad, perfectly vowelled strangers had been preselected as a judging panel, unaware that a decision had already been made. Removed from the need for impeccability, she decided to be truly herself and stitch outrage all over the table.

Roars, but roars of laughter over every

idiosyncratic piece of whimsy she fed them about the deep north.

'You're a good scout, old thing,' he commented afterwards in the cab taking her back to the nasty boarding house across the river. 'Don't take it too hard, there's a good girl.'

'Take what too hard?'

For a moment he looked offended. 'The marriage thing. I did think . . . oh well, on reflection I couldn't handle it. Knew I couldn't. Liquor talking. Leopards not changing and all that. Not fair to you. Not fair at all.'

She said, momentarily spiteful for his dragging it on and on, 'You must write marvellous telegrams.'

But he missed it.

As she prepared to get out of the cab she wondered should she offer the most sisterly of kisses, in return for the siccative quality of his conversation, or merely shake hands. She did neither. She leaned back through the cab window, not caring whether the driver heard or not.

'The difference,' she said, 'between animals and humans is bizarre, don't you think? Humans who are supposed to be rational think of their genitals and their genital needs incessantly while animals, supposed to be irrational, give them no thought at all. Think about it.'

Anyway, she decided, her back turned, herself walking smartly away, the cabbie wouldn't know what the hell genitals were. He'd have ten other words for them.

Later there were letters attempting self-vindication — for what? for what? — and Kathleen, remembering that now, saw phrases that flashed out of the paper . . . one as young and lovely, yes lovely . . . deserves better . . . unable to cope.

A pity, she found herself muttering into the slime of the now cold cappuccino. I might have enjoyed rocking to Europe as the captain's lady, shades of the old Somerset Maugham, in that cabin all spit and polish like an exclusive club. Blackballed, she thought.

Where are you now? she asked the torpid air of the mall fifty years on. Where?

She raised her cup, jerked it in the smallest of toasts to a vanished — was wooer the word? — something — and said aloud, 'Here's to you, Benjamin!', not knowing she had got the name wrong.

Anyway, it had made it easier to accept Ronald.

Who had notions, fantasies, more like it, he
could not sustain in postwar Brisbane, that
exhausted town just emerging from the black-
out and the rationing, its streets still pocked
with urine-stinking bomb shelters, still emo-
tionally reverberating with memories of vanished Yank troops. War brides packed the
departing ships.

Ronald's father returned to the Solomons
to rebuild his trading store in Naghoniara, the
place of the east wind, not on that ravaged site
of so many memories in Tulagi. He was a
goer, a mover. He established a branch store in
Townsville and told his son, 'I want you there,
lad. In any case it's your wife's home town.'
(How could he know she had longed for escape?)

'You handle the mainland end and I'll cope with the rest. You know how it's done.'

Mr Hackendorf senior was still fearsome at sixty-five. His bullying moustaches and red-faced bluster made the two of them feel like schoolchildren, especially Ronald, who was ridden by a sentimental flaw that prevented his ever rebuffing parental demands; for he loved the old man who had brought him up single-handed from the time he was five.

'Where was your mother?' Kathleen asked.

'She ran off with a diplomat,' Ronald said. 'What a laugh!'

Back again! She could have wept!

In that northern coastal town sprawled under its guardian rock their marriage stumbled from the unknown to the boringly too-well-known in a rented timber house on Stanton Hill. Through louvres watching the louvred sea or helping out at the trading store, until the birth of their son put an end to that. Kathleen saw her husband shrink among the stacks of cookers, gas-run refrigerators, sacks of flour and seed, the endless shelving of canned fruits and meat (Dak pork in natural juice, Dak devilled ham, Dak pâté de foie), the coolers and jugs, the automatic oil water heaters, the copra dryers, generators and low watt-consumption ceiling fans with high air displacement.

'Like some unnatural poem,' she had

commented, reading a consignment list aloud on an evening full of moths. Ronald refused to smile.

Was it she who strained the relationship, with her uncivil clutch at truth or truth's flippant side? In a decade when women were supposed to have no opinion at all, she had plenty that she voiced, unabashed, despite the judgemental eyes of other town wives (but then she had been 'blooded' by the captain of the *Fort Caribee*!), not boisterously, mark you, but assuredly.

Add laughter. That's what many found hard to forgive, that plundering effect of mirth.

The truth was she missed Daisy, Daisy now married and moved to Charco where her no-hoper husband ran a supply truck between there and Reeftown and, if she read accurately between the lines of Daisy's scribbled letters, kept her regularly pregnant and beat her up.

Whoops a Daisy!

When Shamrock was born two years after Brian she felt even more trapped, as the heat shrank the four of them in that sluggish town beside the sluggish river. The store and the demands of the store became an Aztec god exacting her husband's heart. Drudgery plundered hers. So it was with relief she heard Ronald announce, not long after his son's sixth birthday, that his father wanted him back in Honiara to take over the business there.

'He's getting on,' he explained, conciliat-
ing, as they sat on their veranda after tea
watching lights bud on the lower slopes and sea
waters turn grey along with the night-dark hills
of their own island. The mosquitoes gave them
no peace. 'He's ill, poor bugger. He needs me.
I can easily get someone to take over this end.'

She could not repress the delight in her
voice.

'At last. We'll be going, too, won't we?
Me and the kids?'

'You've always been nagging for a change.
Here's your chance.'

She could see him now, as she sat in the
mall, see him chasing his never-satisfied dream
of blue water. Poor Ronald. He was to die twice,
in a way.

Before the Burns Philp Line motor vessel,
Tulagi, even reached that reborn town (which
once bore the same name) in the path of the
east wind, old Mr Hackendorf, trader and island
hand, had been laid to rest. His house on
Lengakiki Ridge stood gasping in its own garden jungle of croton and hibiscus, which flow-
ered riotously day after day, leaves and bloom

almost blotting out a gaspingly beautiful view
of the sea, Savo Island and the humped backs
of the Floridas.

The European population was a small,
closed strata-ridden group of a few hundred
mainly government functionaries, among whom
the social pecking order was maintained to an
exotic degree. Kathleen, overcome by an even
more savage heat and by views, wondered
whether she would survive. The beauty was
crushing.

Hospitality was extended in carefully
graded courtesy. The power group had to close
ranks, Ronald kept explaining, against the indi-
genes, who could get above themselves. After
all, the settlers had endured the troubles caused
by Marching Rule and a splinter Christian group
known as Holy Mama, dissidents who threatened the carefully woven colonial fabric of gov-
ernor and governed. Whenever Kathleen asked
about them, the response was heated, indignant
or dismissive but rarely detailed, and her
amusement at the name of the breakaway religious sect brought cool stares of disapproval.

'But the name!' she protested to Ronald.
'It's wonderful! I could join a group with a name
like that!'

'You don't know what you're talking
about,' he said coldly. 'And please, don't say

things like that in public. People will think you're crazy.'

What people?

There were luncheons and dinners to welcome the new chaps.

One splendid affair was at the still thatched-roofed Government House on the shores of Ironbottom Sound.

'You laugh too damn much,' Ronald had complained petulantly afterwards in the house on the ridge. The rooms trembled with the native drums his father had been collecting for years. Harmonics pulsated from skins.

'Roast lamb!' Kathleen had cried. 'Mint sauce!' And she laughed again. 'It was ninety in the shade.'

She was unable to stifle her giggles. 'Scarlet cummerbunds on those poor natives. Surrogate butlers!'

Ronald left her laughing over a gin and tonic and went to check the children. Only the week before, at an informal gathering in the home of one of the assistant secretaries, she had given a spirited version of 'I never forget I'm a lady' on an instrument untuned by salt air and which had only ever shivered beneath easier Schumann. The men had loved it. It was the wives.

She could be left friendless, Ronald worried, sweating over his father's incomplete accounts in the store by the Matanikau River. She would have no back-up. In the islands you needed back-up. He could barely cope with the forest of paper work bequeathed by his father. The Gilbertese native clerk was hopeless but, Ronald decided, hunting excuse, the old man never had the worry of wife and kids. Well, except for him.

He began shelving important work at the store, reporting in late, locking up early and taking the afternoon off. He spent more time with his son, driving out on the island's main road as far as Visale. The small boy was fascinated by the canoes, especially the great ocean-going ones made of bent planks held together by the toughest of thwarts and a resin gum. The sterns curved gracefully high.

'Like the bow of a gondola,' his father explained.

'What's a gondola?'

Ronald told him, and in an old encyclo-paedia on the mouldering bookshelves up at the house, found pictures of Venetian gondoliers languidly idling by their craft. The boy couldn't look at them enough. Yet the big black war canoes frightened him with their bows raised, challenging the terrifying swan neck of the stern. The pearl inlay dazzled. In the smaller craft shark heads were carved, whose pearl teeth could rip approaching enemies. There were nightmares for a while and Kathleen, who lost a lot of sleep from the fruit of this bonding, sat up beside the sweaty tossing kid, damping his forehead down every now and then with a wrung-out flannel, murmuring him back to sleep.

Ronald sat up half the night reading.

Where had all the courting gone? The tenderness?

Daisy's blackened eyes at least showed interest!

She was too realistic to mourn for long that lost, slender, diffident young man with the quirky humour, who had become over the years a tensed sales clerk with the distant crazed eyes of a visionary unable to satisfy his yearnings.

'I was the eaten one,' she would say unfairly, 'during those lost weeks without him.'

'Where's Dad?' Brian (he was called Brian then) had asked, had pestered that year for those three missing weeks in the shadowy house on Lengakiki Ridge outside the town of the east wind. The house held only shadows now of the fierce old man who had died before their arrival. Cupboards were still crammed with shirts and moleskins developing mildew, clothing Ronald was too sentimental to throw out. They had been in this rebuilt town for six months when her husband had taken his first mad decision.

'Where's Dad?' the small boy nagged.

Kathleen was beyond grief with the demands of young children, and besides was at last sorting and discarding the useless belongings of her father-in-law.

'He's been eaten, darling,' she had answered abstractedly, coping with rotting stock, checking the store between times and placating dissatisfied customers. She had argued with him before he had pursued his daft whim, setting out the imponderables. He was sullen about it.

'It's something I've wanted to do for years.'

'And what's that?'

He told her Mount Makarakombou was two thousand four hundred and forty-seven metres high. Don't forget the seven. Or eight thousand and twenty-six feet. Approximately. Don't forget the six.

'Why there?' she had asked mildly.

'Because it bloody is,' Ronald had replied testily. He eyed the hurt on her face. 'It's late payback. Historic payback. My grand-uncle was murdered near Tetere at the end of the century, just for wanting to climb Tatuve. He was with a group of gold fossickers, poor sods.'

'You've picked the wrong mountain,' she said. She couldn't resist smiling.

'This one's higher.'

It had become popular to find bits of abandoned war wreckage clinging to jungle trees like metal rag; to hunt for wing-flaps and engine mountings; to check out identity discs and the decaying detritus of the Pacific war.

'It's not really that either, is it?'

'I'm not looking for plane parts, if that's what you think. I'm settling a score.' He looked embarrassed. 'I'm looking for the new Jerusalem, actually.'

'I hope,' she had said, scrubbing diligently at an imagined spot on the table, 'that you find it. I thought . . .'

'You thought what?'

'Mendana's cross, perhaps. Wasn't it planted in the hills behind Point Cruz? It's a lot closer. You could look for that.'

'My . . . new . . . Jerusalem,' he said, offensively spacing each word, 'is an abstraction. Oh God, what's the use of talking about it.'

There she went trailing her concern for eighteen days into and out of the unhelpful Secretariat, past the Guadalcanal Club, the stores on Mendana Avenue. Officials were irritated and difficult to see, except for the spurious interest of a junior administrative officer who tried to kiss her worry into temporary oblivion. Ronald had left no neat bundle of clothes on the beach.

The store runabout that he had taken had been found three days after he left, washed up in a steamy cove near Inakona.

'Eaten' had worried Brian until his mother explained it had been a joke, dismissing the possibilities of the unknown tempers of *man bush* in regions untouched by *waites*. Unfortunately she compounded his distress by telling jokes about missionaries in cooking-pots. She had always been one for the flip remark, the quick crack! He had screamers of nightmares again for the three weeks before Ronald finally staggered out onto a beach track east of the town. The jungle behind him gave back a huge vegetable yawn. He had lost a great deal of weight and appeared to have difficulty in organising his thoughts. Despite being subjected to intense questioning by the secretary for protectorate affairs, and reprimanded for the trouble he had caused the search parties, he refused to utter one word about where exactly he had been or what had happened.

The island had become for him a bright stamp whose colours had run.

He lost interest in the store. He sat for hours on his veranda looking over the water to Savo Island.

Kathleen hated remembering those days: the gossip at the Club, the quickly dropped eyes and stifled conversations. What was there to do? Eventually an eager Sydney man, who had rolled in like any carpetbagger to suck up chances, persuaded him to sell up both stores, this and the one on the mainland.

What was left but Brisbane?

What was actuality? What fiction?

The pictures came in savagely illuminated splats.

'Regard me,' the junior administrative officer (seconds in Middle English, Oxbridge purr) said between kisses during those troubled weeks, 'as your shrift-father.' Her soggy cheeks were trying to resist his insistent mouth. Any moment the *haus* girl . . .!

Hierarchy had withdrawn its interest; there was no actual offence except idiocy all round. The family left within that month on the *Tulagi*, Kathleen carrying with her sharp pictures of the Joy Biscuit Company building and the Kwong Chow Hotel, but none of the careful suppers of island wives. None of the right places.

Ronald found a paper-shuffling job with a government authority in Brisbane and the ennui, she had to admit, resumed.

Where, Kathleen asked herself in the

windless summers, had vitality fled? There were moments of rapport, brief, barely remembered, when her husband stood by the piano they had bought secondhand from a neighbour, and she played 'Waita Poi' or 'Mandalay' (both versions) or the more robust of the sea shanties, while he sang in a voice now thinning with age. Words and sounds became paradigms for a lost era: 'In the harbour, in the islands, in the Spanish seas,' he carolled in his fine light baritone, 'are the tiny white houses and the orange trees', while the kids cringed with embarrassment as they grew older and her eyes dared not catch his, for fear of uncovering a moist repining beyond bearing.

The long sea-fronting stretch of Mendana Avenue kept dragging its ribbon across her eyes as well, in that hot timber house in the sweltering back streets of Ascot. The mendacity of memory! Ah, the glamour that attached itself, now she was distanced, to those sharky waters round Savo Island, to the junk stores in China-town and the studied luncheons in diplomatic gardens drowning in frangipani. And ah, those tersely accented husbands, the younger of whom stunned the natives when they took their own versions of rowing shells to the lagoon, sculling up and down (*Pull, pull together*, et cetera, et cetera!) to the sombre-eyed interest of beer-guzzling Melanesians, who could have told them a thing or two about canoes predating Boat Day on the Thames!

But here the glamour both enlarged and diminished, as Ronald developed a capacity for silence and lived out the remainder of his days between office and home, both mind and house crammed with South Seas trophies. The crudely carved wooden masks, drums, phalli that his father had collected gave dubious colour to their cul-de-sac purgatory, gave the kids and their schoolfriends the giggles. At weekends Ronald would sit on his wide veranda and stare dismally through a screen of broad leaves, uncomfortable on bamboo, reliving the lotus days of colonialism. He and Kathleen seemed to meet only for the briefest of times. She had begun evening classes; dispiritedly, when he came home from his penitential job, he warmed up the dinner she had left for him (the children were five-day boarders now at schools outside town) and picked at the food without tasting it. If he had only the juice, he would have cried.

His son had surprised him one day during the September holidays as he limped out from the specialist's rooms on Wickham Terrace which he had been visiting for the last few months. Brian was about to be burdened with a special knowledge.

'What is it?' he asked his dad, this tired old man who was still middle-yeared and too young to be so exhausted. In the unrelenting light his father looked sixty, seventy. The September heat was at its most vicious in the four o'clock sun. It was four by all, by every one of the clocks. His father's face was a muddy yellow, too dried out even to sweat. The boy's own shirt was stained across the shoulders and under the armpits with that fresh lively stink of teenage exertion that held legends of cricket and football and swimming, and now of striding, vim-filled despite weather, along the Terrace, arrogantly hoisting a book-satchel. 'What is it?'

His father had swayed on the footpath, caught under the clouting sun and said, 'Don't tell your mother, will you? She'll only worry.'

Gravely the boy promised no.

'It's cancer, son. Not long now, I imagine.'

Three months after that, after his father had finally been forced to retire from the drab job he hated anyway, and with mother guessing at the worst, he had accompanied him to the specialist's rooms whose air was thick with all the stirred dust of a confessional. Tributes to the avernal hung like fog. Sadly he watched his dad rise at the nurse's summons, the too bright red lips of announcement—Doctor's ready for you now!—dropping the article as was done only for God. And he had seen his father stumble, the old man totter a bit, as he limped, a bone cartoon of himself, to the surgery door.

Hadn't mother noticed, for God's sake?

Of course she had. There was a conspiracy of silence, neither wanting to distress the other.

Minutes. Minutes.

The other patients, waiting behind tattered copies of *Woman's Day*, *Newsweek* and *Time*, were becoming edgy: all those failed novenas, rosaries, stations of the cross.

The doctor's face floated like a balloon round the surgery door and a hand summoned him into the sanctum, where he saw Dad, the old man, lying neatly on the examination table, his eyes closed, peacefully asleep.

The boy stood staring. The doctor appeared lost for words.

'I don't know how to say this.' He hesitated.

'Say what?'

'Perhaps I should ring your mother.'

'Mother? Why? What's up?'

The specialist went back to his desk and sat heavily. He would feel safer *ex cathedra*. 'Well, um, look. It's remarkable, really. Quite remarkable. I've never seen anything like it.' He picked up a pen and began tapping, fiddling.

'I examined your father as usual,'—the boy could not take his eyes off the sheet-covered figure on the bench—'and when I'd finished he asked me what the . . . er . . . prognosis, the . . . um . . . situation was. As it were. Do you understand?'

Brian nodded.

'I had to tell him, I'm afraid, that the cancer was incredibly advanced since his last visit a month ago and that there would be no remissions. You were aware he had cancer, weren't you?' Brian was beyond nodding. 'Then . . . and this is what . . .' The specialist rubbed one hand across his forehead, seeking answers. 'He looked up at me, you see. He was still lying there. And then he said, "Right!" and closed his eyes and died.'

It was some monstrous joke.

The silence in the room swelled and added its weight to the soundlessness of the sheeted figure, the stillness of wasted body beneath that sheet.

'Oh geez!' he cried. 'Just like that!'

'I'm afraid so. Look, ask my attendant to ring your mother and see if she can come in. No. Wait. I'll do it.'

The boy went over to his father. The specialist had left the face uncovered, gaunt and in need of a shave.

'Dad?' he whispered hopefully. 'Dad?'

But the eyes were closed against him and tears came. He found himself kneeling on the floor beside the bench, his forehead pressed against his father's uninterested hand, simply saying the monosyllable over and over until eventually the nurse came in from the other room and led him away.

He didn't know what to do. He had crashed head-on into mortality. To wait here for mother? To wait and go with the ambulance? Where? The specialist wasn't much help with his continuing whisper of 'there, son!' and after a while he slipped out of the waiting room, caught a tram back to Ascot and sat on the veranda in his father's old cane lounger, waiting for mother.

She had trudged up the steps an hour later, Shamrock trailing, hauling shopping bags.

'You should have told me,' Kathleen accused, 'that you knew. Before. You should have said.'

'You should have told me,' the boy said. His lips were set stubbornly against the cruelty of the world. Shamrock sobbed in her bedroom for the poor old withdrawn prickly codger, despite everything, despite the arguments, the taciturnity. Despite it all, she sobbed and sobbed.

The boy wasn't prepared for his mother's dry-eyed grief.

'Wouldn't you know!' this old girl said aloud in the heat of the mid-day mall. 'Wouldn't you just *know*!'

Daisy could have been sitting there, for all she knew. Kathleen kept noddling through those last days before Ronald died, the horrible secret of his illness huddled within, unable to turn to the children, lost between voyages in her own port. She drank the last of her coffee angrily, one-swig Kath, and shook her head to free it from all that unhappy stuff. There was a busker under the shopfront just nearby, strumming guitar and singing mournfully about the inland. *Can't sing like my boy*, she thought. *Not a patch on him.*

Just briefly she wondered what Brain would think if he knew she'd come back. But she didn't want him to know, didn't want to push herself in where she wasn't wanted. Anyway, she couldn't find him even if. He was somewhere around, up in the hills.

The busker was packing up his guitar and moving off now. She felt sorry for him. 'No talent,' she muttered to herself, 'poor kid.' He was moving across to the people at the next table, his cap held ready, hoping for a handout. 'Got to give the poor coot something,' she told Daisy, fumbling in her handbag for loose change. 'Daisy, you should have heard Brain in his palmy days.'

She blinked and Daisy vanished. But she went on, talking to air.

There was no doubt: Brian's voice was better than his father's. As the kids grew beyond the stage of scowling shame while father insisted on running through his repertoire of ballads, Kathleen was delighted when occasionally the boy joined them at the piano and sent rich true notes soaring about the living room. He was playing the lead in a school production of *The Gondoliers* and needed the practice. Although he was only fourteen his voice had changed without notice-able cracking and had the mature tenor assur-ance of a man.

The year before she had sat with Ronald at a school concert watching their son as he sang a bracket of Irish songs for Saint Patrick's day. Up there on stage, spotlighted, with his still unfuzzed face, he looked younger than he was, but when his voice, ripe and full and strong, lofted 'Macushla' and 'Mother Machree' to the soaring roof of the hired theatre, that stunning opposition of school shirt and matinee idol voice had the crowd cheering and pulping their palms. God has been good to him, the Brothers said in the foyer at interval. He has a great gift.

'You heard what Brother said,' Kathleen repeated many times later, absorbed in savour-ing the words. 'A great gift. Your father and I are very proud.'

'I've made the second fifteen,' Brian said. He could think of nothing else.

'Nothing else,' she had complained to Daisy. 'The one thing he could do really well and never worked at. Oh it was a pleasant enough ... hobby, I suppose. But he sang to please himself. "That's what it's for, Mum," he used to say. "There's more to life than that." '

She could hear him now, taking a pair of sparkling eyes to the delight of parents driven down the old Sandgate Road for school play night, encored to a reprise, *sotto voce*, and feel still the tears of pride that made her look away and squeeze Ronald's fevered hand.

Had she but world enough and time, she reflected in the peopled barrenness of the mall, she would invent the ultimate preservative for those makeshift, rough and ready, short-lived moments.

Instinctively she put her hand to her face, touching the remnants of what time had left her.

She was falling apart.

Cutting loose.

Doing the unexpected.

Kathleen craved some moment of consequence in what had become a treadmill existence as she steered her children through adolescence. *I don't count*, she had written to Daisy still sweating it out in Charco, *those child-*

*hood traumas of measles, mumps and chicken-pox.
Or the mindless food-hunt, the cooking, eating and
expelling the stuff just so the whole damn cycle can
start again. (Hey, that's a laugh, isn't it?) I don't
place much stress on rows at the office, promotion,
retirement. Where's the buzz?*

She had made room for one of those
moments the year after Ronald died, tugged by
sentiment, perhaps, or simply the need to flee
the mundane while her children were safe in
boarding school. Amazing herself, she took a
week's leave and went back to the town of the
east wind, flying in where once, eleven years
before, she had arrived by inter-island trader.
When the plane came down over Guadalcanal,
the jungled heights of the island, fold upon fold
of uncontrolled vegetable growth, seized and
choked her mind. She saw Ronald, or imagined
she could see him, clambering, hacking, crawl-
ing through implacable forest to sate an obses-
sion. His thin white figure in starched drill
and toupee, all the tropic duds, kept vanishing
and reappearing, heading ever towards what
she guessed to be the summit of Mount
Makarakombou.

Nothing had changed. A lot had changed.
In the still familiar bar of the hotel on
Mendana Avenue the past swept in. She had
told no one she was going, not even the chil-

dren, and now layer upon layer of time peeled her naked.

In the harbour, in the islands, in the Spanish seas, Ronald's voice sang in the highest reaches of her skull as she walked during each of the next few days past Government House and the Secretariat to the Guadalcanal Club, where she rediscovered the junior administrative officer, redder, stouter, and now an assistant secretary. There was not a kiss in sight.

'Have I changed that much?' She resented the bleating sound as she jogged his memory.

'Married man these days,' he countered, self-protectively. 'Three beaut kids. You'll meet the wife later on. She's dropping by for a drink. God, Kathleen, what a turn up, eh? Why didn't you let anyone know you were coming? We could have turned it on for you.' He was convivial with a gin sling. 'Not many of the old team left, I'm one of the few who stayed on.'

'You knew about Ronald, I suppose.'

'Yes. Sorry, Kath. Always liked the old boy. Do you know . . . just a few days before you left, after the store was sold, he told me what happened that time he went missing.'

Kathleen found herself staring into her glass, afraid to urge.

'Yes,' the assistant secretary said, 'he reached the top all right. And he managed to cut his name and the date on a boulder up there. It's true. Went up to see it for myself a year later. It was on the way back he got bushed. Bad show, really. All of it.'

Crazily she believed then that it was Ronald she had seen from the spy-hole of the descending plane, living and reliving his moment of glory in that steaming wilderness of tree and vine. Nostalgia made her want to weep again, even after a year, especially after a year, grabbed by the stupidity of his pluckiness, whose driving folly she had never understood.

She finished her drink, leaving the assistant secretary sitting there, and walked up the hill to the house on the ridge. The temptation to knock, to court invitation, jabbed as she surveyed the familiar lines of veranda, the garden denser but much the same, brilliant with scarlet blossom on the poinciana trees. She turned and looked across to Savo Island, unchanged in unchanging waters, her back exposed now to the pointed words that still flew about those rooms. She winced under ghost barbs.

If she could, she would have redrawn the maps of those lost times, overcome by sadness and its high dingo howl across emptied, flattened desert-scapes. She thought of her children and their kid faces became mnemonics for domestic detail she now dug up, gently sifting earth and sand, to lay each moment out as if it were a bowl, vase, tile, of simple but searing beauty.

History was more nostalgia than facet. Correction, than fact: an aggregation of personal moments with their sickening lurches of love and hate.

As she sat alone that night in the dining room of the Hotel Mendana, the black waiter asked curiously and, she imagined, reprovingly, 'Where is your husband?'

She looked up and smiled and took her time responding. 'Where is your wife?'

Giggling, he backed away, all stumbling feet and flaphands, from this cheeky *waite*.

She went on picking at her omelette, wondering if, for Ronald's sake, she should have mentioned he had left his mark on the summit of one of their highest peaks.

Where, after all, *was* her husband?

The best thing, she supposed, about that week was knowing no one knew where she was. The boundary lines of protocol were still drawn on the island, though by shakier hands, and the supper party the assistant secretary organised for her at his home was a terrible mix of stiff and hearty, through all of which the secretary's wife regarded her with sharp and curious eyes nourished by the gossip that still, after all this time, gave transfusions of energy. *Nothing*, should she explain loudly over the canapés, *beyond sweat and arms and unwanted kisses in the sticky afternoons of those three lost weeks*?

The temptation to say loudly, clearly, 'There was no *pus-pus*, my dear,' shocking with the unacceptable pidgin obscenity, almost overcame her. A nauseous wave swept her up and out to the bathroom where she was noisily sick for quite some time.

I've cut and run, she wrote on a card for Daisy. The card showed native huts and women in brightly coloured Mother Hubbards. *Wasn't going to tell a soul but I've decided cutting and running is what it's all about. I think the kids have inherited that gene from me!*

Got your card, Daisy remembered when they next met years later. *You old devil, you*.

Daisy was without envy, never said 'half your luck' or 'wish I'd been there', never stained the moment.

'*I'm* lucky,' she always said. '*You're* lucky. Watched any telly lately? If you have you'll *know* you're lucky.'

Daisy put her right, letting her see the brevity of the programme, the limited number of items, the transience of applause.

Here's to you, Daise! Cheers!

'Let's go back a little,' she said to Daisy, mumbling away to herself in the mall. 'I want to tell you about them, about the kids. Your turn next week. That *Brain*!' she said. 'That *Shamrock*!'

Now yearning for the confidences, the shared comfort of age, she would write Daisy long letters full of plaint. Goodbye. Goodbye to those years in which she huddled in the same house, always the same, while son and daughter flapdoodled their way through Mickey Mouse humanities courses on straight C's.

Herself unsurprised, still on the secretarial game but translated, now she also had put a course or two behind her, into something a little more meaningful as a parliamentary worker, learning to keep her too ready lips closed, ploughing ahead to retirement down the track with only the occasional flirtation in sight. Dollops of carelessly dropped, scented dross, she told herself and also another elderly prospective escort who promptly, promptly . . . and, my God, there was a further not so fragrant deposit littering the fence marge.

So who cares? cared? She had the kids, no longer kids, to worry about in the bleak evenings, wondering how straight C's and humanities establish themselves and their holders in the expanding early sixties except in protest flings with mounted police or in baton-beaten greenie marches. There had been narrow squeaks with alternative communes seductively beckoning. Shamrock had taken a year off to find herself.

'Where will you look, dear?' Kathleen had
asked mildly.

'Oh Jesus, you do crap me off!'

I lived through that, Kathleen admitted,
through all that sulky acrimony, that impudent
flouncing, until Shamrock hitched her way to a
commune outside Mackay, an outwardly dec-
orously run family group that, according to a
chastened and returned daughter, was organised to punishment point by a failed law student with stunning connections in the state
judiciary. Daddy had funded the farmlet, a pre-
postmodernist remittance gesture. There was
much regimentation her unaccommodating
daughter had resisted. The male/female balance
was preserved by rostered swapping. A kind of
tremor, Sham insisted, ran through the group
every Monday when the new copulation sched-
ule was pinned to the breakfast-room notice
board. Culture, too, was regulated. You will
learn oboe. You will play bassoon. You will
mould pots, paint, weave, wood-carve. But
above all you will sleep with James, with Trevor,
with Russell. You will help build the hayshed
and do the washing and cooking every third
day. (Hey, don't the *men* get a go?) You will
learn ballet, sleep with Shark, do the . . .
Shamrock lasted only two months and revealed
these things to her mother in later dribbles of

self-pitying confession. Her small face seemed permanently morose. There was a poignant squalor about her and about the disciples she described, whose earnings on regular week-day jobs and/or unemployment benefits vanished into an unaudited bank account for the failed law student, who did at least know dollars and which way to butter his bread.

In the seventh week she had announced rudely that she was utterly tired of beansprouts and would, she swore, remember to her last breath the crocodile-eyed law failure (I *mean*, mother, how can you fail at *law*?) making hip roofs of his tapering unworked fingers and saying, 'I'm not sure, Shamrock, whether you fit in with the ideology of our little family, whether you have assimilated the philosophic concepts of the group. Some of your partners . . . that is, your sexual partners . . . have complained about a lack of enthusiasm, of an . . . how shall I put it? . . . inert compliance.'

She had said, 'I will truly vomit if I don't get my jaws round a hunk of steak, medium rare.'

Shamrock had married before the necessity to work had claimed her, ironically enough, another lawyer who had given up his practice to enter parliament and whom Kathleen immediately dubbed the minister for transports.

'This makes me wonder about the ulti- mate charity of fate,' Kathleen whispered to Brain as they stood with fixed smiles in Cathedral gloom waiting for Shamrock to be legally joined to her ambitious backbencher. Despite the many junctions before the religious ceremony, Shamrock flaunted herself in glaring white, tossed bouquets to prismatic brides- maids, caught Brain's mocking eye and fast- bowled him with a posy. Blush. Giggle. At the city hotel reception, in a spate of clichéd well wishes and lewd telegrams, she kissed her mother sparingly on the cheek and then van- ished on a Barrier Reef honeymoon without a word of thanks.

'For what?' she might have asked if prod- ded. 'For this pagan mockery?' Now Kathleen merely writhed uneasily, trapped in a clawing landscape.

She was paying off the loan for the wed- ding for the next three years. That girl, she told herself, can't even spell matrimony without an 'e'.

'Can't seem to get my act right, Mum,' Brain moaned. 'What the hell goes wrong?'

'Don't look at me!' his mother said.

After university he had been offered the management of a motel in the far north by a friend of a friend. The motel closed a year later. He became a working partner on a prawn boat and was deckhand, odd-jobber and mainte-nance johnny. He had to keep assuring himself he was expanding his abilities, stretching his limits. One burning, slashing day in the Gulf at the height of the season, the refrigeration plant failed. Nothing he did could save the catch, not even red-eyed panic. The stench around the body. The business lost over fifty thousand dollars on that one disastrous trip.

He moved to Townsville where, brooding in the choking air of a Belgian Gardens flat during a strike by sanitary workers, he mentally perfected the notion of solidifying dunny contents in a kind of Araldite so that the entire pan appeared as some exotic dish set in aspic. He found no backers. Peughh! Urk! Nutter!

People were beginning to laugh at each new proposal. He had lost nearly all his small savings.

The minidepression.

The boom.

Nascent charm saved him.

Bosie was an accident, a fleshing of the fantasies of sweat-filled solitary nights, a come-by-chance at a luncheon in a very expensive seafood restaurant in Brisbane where he had returned to complain to Kathleen and lick his financial wounds. The restaurant was the latest trendy place to be seen. Diners were neither put off nor rendered vomitous by the window's street decoration of a monster two-foot carp floating listlessly in a tank six inches longer than its body and suppurating slowly in its own juices, despite the languid efforts of a pump and a few strings of watergrass.

From the table behind. Bosie managed to spray her future husband with a laughter-disgorged mouthful of peppery riesling. Apologies, little wipings, flutterings. Vowels so rounded they almost, but only almost, came out flat. It was too tedious, Brain—for the name started not long after that, snapped up by mother with crude guffaws—decided in later years. And horribly inevitable. *My God!* he often murmured to himself. *Crook wine at midday! We both had it coming.*

She was the daughter of a speculator who had made a killing selling swamplands for housing estates near the Gold Coast and who had conveniently died, leaving everything to his doted-upon child. For a time his financial agonies were eased. But he had reckoned without his wife's spending abilities. Bosie (after two years he had forgotten her birth name) had private-school assumptions as well as desperate elocution. Within three years they had two pouting, aggressive, indulged boys who were later rendered semiliterate under the new tolerance curricula promoted by academic refugees from the classroom.

That was all it took. (Was that all it took?)

Marriage was the dangled worm that hooked women. Women were the dangled worms that hooked men. Both ways it was a bad deal, a lousy deal. Who was trapped the most? He found awe-inspiring those decades of small miscalculations, the trifles on which monstrous disasters depended: the struggle for home ownership—but the right sort of home!—the home that would bring Bosie's ultimately suburban approval; the children—those beaking birds querulous with demand; the school fees; the debts; the overdraft. That never-ending overdraft. The pretence, at gatherings of friends who were also engaged in pretending, that everything was jake, hunky-dory, keen, cool, a total gas. Cheap laughter around the unpaid-for pools with the cheap wine flowing and in the back of every mind, thrust back but there, the tick of the plastic card meter, tocking over.

Hey, what a party!

Great bash, man!

Jesus, Brain, do I have a hangover!

Smashing, Bosie darling. Absolutely smashing. We had a ball! Just loved those thingummies en croûte. You must tell me how you did them.

Make it our place next time.

And ours.

And ours.

And ours and ours and ours and . . .

In the red. In the mood and in the red. A frieze of unpally bank managers. In the red but still in the mood. Failed projects one after another. Even failed despair. In the syncopated pauses Brain pondered suicide, thoughts flippant enough of cutting out without a trace; of leaps from buildings, train hurlings, boat plungings. He couldn't crack even those and Bosie's *Oh Brain, must you! Bims and Chaps are at boarding school. Think of them.* changed to *Thank God Bims and Chaps are at boarding school. Thank God they're spared seeing their father* . . . (But seeing his father, that grotesque scene in the specialist's rooms on the Terrace as a horrible entr'acte before he too moved on to the next scheme, to collapse in a torpor of weather when the induced lassitude of Brisbane's streets threatened to choke.)

He was not really serious, Bosie assured telephoning friends who had heard of his latest financial misadventure, a disco called Heart of Darkness with shares largely owned by the minister for transports and closed down after three months by the police, who wanted more protection money. *If he were truly serious*, she babbled, *then he would achieve oblivion. Listen, why don't we meet for coffee?*

Huh?

Bosie punished him.

'I've booked it up,' she would say challengingly to his outraged face (there were no cheapskate kisses these days!) as he glared at a new dishwasher, freezer, airconditioner, inflatable swimming-pool table, entire new summer wardrobe.

'You've bloody what?'

Shit! Head between hands. Oh shit!

It felt, Brain decided in his saner moments, like the Hundred Years War. And the protagonists never changed. *The woods decay,* he quoted softly and sullenly to himself, pouring fibre bran into his breakfast bowl, *the woods decay and fall, the vapours weep* (pouring the milk) *their burthen to the ground . . . Me only cruel immortality consumes.* ' "I wither," ' he suddenly shouted at the heavenly morning glittering on the impeccable surface of the pool, ' "slowly in thine arms, here at the quiet limit of the *world*!" '

'Brain, the neighbours!' Bosie cried, coming out to the kitchen.

Yet, ' "And thee returning on thy silver heels," ' he mischanted impertinently to her after one particularly trying evening with a failed avocado grower from the Tablelands.

'What?' Bosie snapped. 'What? I haven't the faintest idea what you're talking about.'

'No matter. No matter at all.'

He knew and Alfred Lord T. knew exactly what he meant.

He would observe Bimbo and Chaps home for what Bosie called the hols or later, the vac, wincing from her stagey pretentiousness that drove them inevitably into displays of boorish retroaction. Yet I am a natural lout, he would admit after sottish evenings. The boys have my genes. Or half of them. You didn't will their gawky insolence or sullen response to the best-will-in-the-world inquiries. You simply watched the bad manners prickle out like acne.

Against which his wife waged increasingly refined battle, chiding them in vowels so ovate the boys paused physically within a smidgin of being flattened another way.

Cor!

1992.

His marriage had endured two decades.

They had moved north on the promise of nirvana. More hotel management in booming Reeftown, the man with the fake sincere glance had persuaded. Needs people like you. People of your calibre with get up and go. You can't miss. Not these days. Not in this economic climate. Simply can't miss.

Could he not?

PR for Reef Tours. That lasted longer. Bosie had chosen their house after cutting a swathe through soon-disaffected real estate agents —another year, another mortgage—at one of Reeftown's northern beaches, a low-slung, rambling affair turned in on itself (*Like us*, Brain had hissed) and away from the street, the living room a spacious, roofed, unwalled affair surrounding a pool of extravagant blue. Bosie was ecstatic. There were parties parties parties, backgrounded by hi-fi joy from carbuncular speakers depending like enormous ripe plums from the pergola roof. 'Or haemorrhoids,' coarse Brain suggested, inspecting the completed work. 'Brain!' his wife had cried. 'For God's sake! Must you reduce . . .'

The only thing Bosie failed at was words.

More plans sprouted and withered. There were months of riches on paper followed by financial drought. Backers for improbable business projects came and went. They went bad-tempered. There were more parties and more dinners, more luncheons by the pool and in it. God! What a rage! There was political involvement followed by political accusation followed by withdrawal of funds.

Twenty years' endurance.

Fair enough, was his summation. Fair enough. The boys were more or less self-sufficient except for those lean times when they reappeared with dollar signs in their eyes.

'You're not the only one who wants freedom,' Bosie had said bitterly. 'Why do men think they are the only ones trapped? And the only ones entitled not to miss the great world out there, eh?'

'We're both trapped, love.' He was conscious of vast sadness for them both. 'Both. I know exactly how you feel because it's how I feel. It's simply a question, isn't it, of who's going to be the first to make a break for the wall.'

Bosie glanced up with suddenly fearful eyes. She was unequipped for any sort of career now, her pert good looks vanishing along with those outdated office skills she had once sported. She was fit only for counter-jumping. She mentioned these facts, ground them out reluctantly, acidly, the data of those decades.

'But why not?' Brain was unfeeling. 'Why not get a job?'

'There are no jobs, haven't you noticed? It's impossible to get a job even slinging hash. You damn well know that. I've spent years organising dinners and parties to foster your hare-brained projects and now I'm on the heap.'

She hated admitting that, hated the pencillings of age that scrawled the indifferent interest of time.

'But you enjoyed them.'

'Enjoyed what?'

'The parties, those Goddamn endless dinners. You played at the sweet life. Why didn't you get off your bum when the kids were at school and do a course? Retrain. Something. You had the bloody time.'

There was no answering that.

Bosie heaved a lilo into the pool and stalked off. Brain heard her car (the second car!)

start up and then the engine's rage fading along the bay front. He expelled his held breath contentedly.

Ultimately he wanted to be alone. Alone alone alone.

Yet he failed to achieve even that.

Bosie, sobbing her grievances into the eager ears of pals weak in wisdom but brimming with advice and hoping, perhaps, to cobble up her frayed marriage, was persuaded to book Brain and herself onto a group discovery tour of Europe.

What an innocent!

Part Two

*P*olice report being called to the aid of an elderly man found collapsed in a Reeftown park late yesterday afternoon.

The man, who is in his eighties, insists that he comes from Melbourne and has no recollection of how he got to Reeftown. Locals say he had been observed sitting on the same bench on the Esplanade for two days.

Disoriented and suffering from exposure, he had his first name pinned to his shirt but appeared not to recognise it. 'Albert' is 160 centimetres tall, of slight build. He is crippled in one leg and is partly deaf.

Anyone able to help in identifying him is asked to contact the Elder Care Group, Reeftown, where he is being looked after.

Reeftown Herald, *10 July 1990*

WHOOPSADAISY! DAISY had said, stumbling on the kerb edge in Adelaide Street.

The two old girls had linked arms for support as they crossed to the big store.

God, how she missed Daisy these days. It had been good for those years when she had come down from the north hutched in some hot-box in Shorncliffe. Good for that surprise of hearing Daisy's voice crackling over the telephone wires in unexpected announcement.

'There could only be one Hackendorf,' she had cackled. 'Knew I'd find you.'

All those years. Great groping palm hands of alocasia had fumbled gloomily towards their meeting place on the footpath, just above the stairs to the conveniences. 'Where are all your kids, now, Daisy?' she had asked. 'Buggered off!' Daisy told her. 'Perth. Melbourne. You name it. On me own now.' Daisy with her streaks of carrot still showing through the untended grey mop, her cheap floral cottons displaying those creped arms and age-spotted skin, her most precious belongings shoved into a plastic shopping bag she never let go. *Not a proper bag lady*, she would say. *Not proper.* Just another desperate from the lonely house she lived in on the shores of Moreton Bay. She'd become obsessive about burglars. 'But I have to get out,' she almost whimpered. 'I can't stay in that poke of a place endlessly.' Of course you can't, Kathleen had assured. 'See,' the other had said, scrabbling down to the bottom of the bag. 'It's just these few things I'm frightened to leave.' Snapshots. All the kids. Her mum. A pensioner bank book. Her health card. A book she'd won for the best composition in primary school. Show me, Kathleen had urged. Do show. *Presented to Daisy O'Brien, Biloela Primary School, 1930.* 'That and the kids,' Daisy said. 'My only achievement. And now I never get to see them, they're too busy. I've got to hang on to something, haven't I?'

All those years meeting at that bus stop and going off to do the cafeterias in the big stores, treating themselves to cream cake and tea, complaining about the thoughtlessness of kids and laughing a lot between complaints and then Daisy didn't show. After their last outing, Kathleen discovered, she had walked behind a backing truck and that was that. Like that! Oh God, Kathleen thought, having a small nightmare: the photos and the prize copy of *We of the Never Never* and the pensioner cards and the savings account with fifty-five dollars put by for emergencies, scattered in Adelaide Street and rammed back into the bag and then thrown away because the ambulance had come and Daisy was silent for keeps.

Hey, Daisy, wherever you are! Listen! Listen to me. It gets better! It's not all grief.

Take five!

    Take longer if you feel like it.

    Here's this crazy, this wacker, this . . . this
. . . whatever you feel like calling the poor coot,
obsessed, no, riddled with this maggot to sing,
golden-throated, golden-tongued, Tosti's last
song, the ultimate lament, from a bridge in
Venice, a bridge spanning one of the smaller
canals leading into the bassino.

    Ah well.

    For a once-off?

    To frighten the gondoliers? The tourists?
Send sonic but useless messages to a lost love?

    Well, maybe.

    Nothing but water and bells, he imagined,

and his voice, rapturous with resonance, rocking the bassino into wavelets.

He lifted his head into dawn air, inhaled
deeply, opened his mouth wide, wider, and
launched into the opening bars of *L'ultima canzone: M'han detto che domani, Nina vi fate sposa*,
he sang. Full. Loud. Louder. Resonance.

Rez-o-nance!

Workmen going by hesitated, grinned
widely, leaned against the bridge railing and
eyed him from under their caps with pleasure.
One joined in. They sang *duetto*, allowing their
voices to melt into curves that floated up and
over the water, dominating the liquidity of bells,
curling into the wisps of cirrus teasing church
spires across that glinting world. His song was
a gondola of grief on which he poled away
from the watchers, even his singing partner,
oblivious to their surprise or delight, sensing
only the rotundity of sound as it left his throat,
curvilinear.

When he reached the last throbbing note
—and he allowed it to throb in the finest Ital-
ianate style—there was a burst of applause,
ragged, fragmented, from the loiterers. '*Grazie*,'
he said with a self-mocking bow. '*Grazie. Molte
grazie.*'

Without looking into their smiles, their
curiosity, he turned and began walking away

quickly, losing himself in a network of alleys and lanes, crossing market squares, moving ever further and further from the hotel where his wife was now unpacking in the too expensive room their travel agent had booked. Leaving now before the old routine set in, the museum trudging, gallery goggling, piazza dining turning each day into its organised monetary orgasm. Bells reached a climax of slashed air all about him, cutting small winds to streamers from a tower across the square; and he chased after their summons and entered a world filled with the cobwebs of ancient prayers.

He was, is, interested in the processes of goodness, the abstractions of duty, self-sacrifice, the sheer purity of the unladen soul. On this morning of early March, striding across the endless skies, as it were, of Venice's floating floor, the sole-heel-toe of him felt no paving, no grit and agonised clutch to earth. As if involved in chicanery, in subterfuge, he had whizzed from that hotel room, scooting across arpeggios of bellringers, silently exhorting steeples, workmen, cringing cats, sly before-times money-changers, insomniac tourists, in order to utter the briefest aspiration of God-directed gratitude.

So long, Bosie!

So long, Bimbo and Chaps!

Bimbo and Chaps now not quite completing academic courses, not quite dropping out.

Bosie unpacking the drip-dry and hanging it carefully on racks in the monstrous wardrobe that threatened the bed.

So long! *Arrivederci!*

A Mass was half-completed, the sanctuary bell ringing at the elevation of the Host, the saddened weathered cunning simple duplicate human discs raised, lowered, raised, the prayers pressed like everlastings between hands draped with rosaries, rings and the tiredest of tired skins.

Kneeling with chin on knuckled hands, he thought of Bosie. Why didn't she laugh? Ever? Once, listening to a political leader gabbling idiotically away on television, he had commented, 'They've left the scrambler on.' Not a smile. Not a glimmer of a smile. She was unmoved by most things of the spirit. And another once when he played her Te Kanawa singing Strauss's *Vier letzte Lieder* with that effortless floating, effortless buoyancy of the heart out of sight, a bird — out — of — sight, ah, she had switched on the Hoover and worked around his scuffed running shoes. There was nothing like the Romantics, he had informed her, talking to air. The hell, he had told her, with Victorian schmaltz and tenors, me dear, one hand lightly placed on the grand, moustache always blond

down-drooping, thrumming to the tentative
occasionally wrong notes struck by an hour-glass
garbed woman-fashion, swaying on the piano-
stool. She had kept on Hoovering. But Tosti!
Brain had begun to shout above the racket.
Who could resist him? He couldn't. Partly for
the thought of that ingratiating Latin giving
music lessons to the royal toad and the toad's
children in the soot and gas lamps of London.

His own eyes were stained with the sea as
he explained.

Jesus God! *L'ultima canzone!* He would
try not to remember that it was written at
Folkestone.

He flicked off the player and began singing to his Hoovering wife.

The last song.

Over

and

over.

'For Chrissake!' Bosie had screamed, going
out to the pool and an aureole stench of guinea
flower. 'Will you give up on that Goddamn
song! That bloody song!'

'Mother,' he had reprimanded, following
his wife and breaking from lyric mode to speech
mid-note, 'played it for Father.'

'I don't,' Bosie shouted, her small acquisi-
tive face screwed up into what Brain recog-

nised as the first honest resentment in twenty
years of marriage, 'give a stuff if she played it
for the president of the Yew Ess of Ay or Yas-
ser Arafat.' A leaf dropped its exclamation
point, tested her hair briefly and fluttered away
to the terrace.

That vignette he offers now to his raw
and guilty soul. Or had he screamed slut? He
couldn't remember.

He was hugging his personal alto rhap-
sody to himself like a comforter, a warmer, a
cuddle-bunny of escape into unachieved but
dreamt-of contacts, say: girl crossing landscape—serious, gawky—on a lonely beach on
Magnetic; girl swinging into bus-stumble, his
quickly gallant hand supporting a succulence
of flesh, wanting, oh God, wanting what? He
could accept the lust in either vignette with
the figure erased from landscape.

Was he a queer?

Years ago—three? four?—Nina Waterman had knelt literally at his feet on a pool
scootway flooded by the splashings of yoicks,
polluted by arcadian flat-chested nymphs and
lugger shepherd boozers, and bowed her mag-
nificent head as his party song climaxed: *honey,
did yo' hear dat mockin' bird sing las' night?* To
lager and stubby wash of the good ship Hackendorf, Brain Hackendorf sang.

When he left the church the gondolas on the canal swung by with barely a glance from boatered polesters under the thin wash of early sun damped down by mist, pollution and the rags of sea-dragging cloud.

So long, Bosie, now rinsing out her underwear to hang on a neat packaway traveller's clothesline hooked across bathtub or shower screen.

In a room whose ceiling was cluttered with *putti*.

You brought a new kind of love to me, blooted Harold 'Shorty' Baker on trumpet, mute blocking like a heavy head cold the driving rhythms of Billy Strayhorn and Cue Porter. The ghetto-blaster vibrated with its own racket from a barley-sugar balcony above him and there he goes, there goes Brain, who could not refrain from snapping fingers along with the sound, chuck-chucking as he almost pranced along cobbled streets to meet Nina Waterman, cool and agelessly middle-aging but still yummy, adjusting hat and scarf in the colonnade of a broken-down, still gorgeous palazzo.

Twinned! Snap!

There. Standing half-shaded by portico, by hat, one finger probing a timetable, her timeless profile trapped in connections. Nina. He felt that wild rush of excitement he used to get forty years before when he played hookey.

She had no sense of culpability.

'This,' she would later insist to her divorce lawyer, when she decided long after that divorce might be neater, 'was entirely unplanned. We had been trapped,' she would explain, 'on the same tour. As it were. Ironically . . .' and she had smiled her ancient Attic smile . . . 'a discovery tour. Fifteen days, twelve cities. I ask you!'

They had not lasted with their partners more than two.

'Cities or days?' the lawyer had asked.

'Why, days.'

In Rome Bosie had become sniping, whining in the Pantheon, the Colosseum (he, Brain, was the one spreadeagled on sand under lion's breath!) and in the rain-drizzled square of St Peter's. She craved big spending along the Via Veneto. Mr Waterman developed Roman belly on the first day, a distressing condition that was to affect him for the rest of the tour, whose conductor was relentless in his insistence on culture. He barely noticed his wife had gone, and when Bosie bitterly pointed out to him on the third morning that some conclusion could be drawn by both absences, he cheered up immediately despite his illness.

'This,' Brain said to Mrs Waterman, touching her hand as it rested on a stone balustrade of their fourth crumbling church on day one, 'is not what I really came for.'

'The decay?'

Joke, she had explained to his hurt, blunt features. Blunted as when he had pleaded with Bosie for God's sake just to hear Schreier singing his guts/heart out for a minute, half a minute, in the *Schwanengesang* and had said *Hist*! Actually, he had said, 'Hey! Lissen a that!' as once, three years before he had held a rapt finger to the tip of Johnny Hodges' fluid lace of notes and caught a barely known Nina Waterman watching with poised amusement. Bosie had poked out her tongue and walked away, slamming a muffling door between them. Dampered! Twice!

'That's for all of us, the decay,' he said. And her time-endangered hand twitched on eroded stone.

87
•
Coda

The leaving had been easier than he could have imagined, having imagined so often these last years in the humid nights of Reeftown with his wife snoring persistently beside him. Take five. Take this: an abandoned heap of outer garments (holding memories of his vanished dad) on the dazzle strip of some deserted beach, any beach, and a two-hundred-yard swim round a point to predeposited dry clothing, cash and a motor-bike panting to whip him away, never, not ever, to be found as Brain Hackendorf again.

The reality was the briefest note tucked under a bedside lamp, his pockets stuffed with air ticket, travellers' cheques and passport with numerous visas already stamped in and throbbing to be used in rhythm with his overexcited middle-aged heart.

Mere escape, he argued.

Or was it the sight of Nina Waterman, more a metaphor of escape than a fornicatory goal, under the ambiguous shelter of her dipping hat?

It was, he insisted inwardly, giving her cool fingers a belated squeeze, the escape itself.

Bimbo and Chaps would be outraged, but not for long.

Kathleen would be amused.

He must send a card to that sweltering
Brisbane home. That's if the poor old girl could
take it all in, she was so damn vague these days.
Vague and forgetful. He must ask Shamrock if
she ever wet the bed. He'd heard that was an
early sign. Incontinence of brain and bladder.
But would Shamrock, entangled with the enter-
tainment schedules of her ambitious backbencher husband, even have bothered to visit
the old Mum in months unless she needed
something? Shamrock had never been a daugh-
terly daughter or for that matter a sisterly sister, any more, he had to admit, than he had
been a son.

He blinked away guilt brought back by
dubious wall stains and puddles along the alley-
ways and focused on his partner in elopement.
His conscience wouldn't let him alone.

Something nagged.

Guilt.

Impulsively he rang Kathleen from a pay
phone at an *ufficio postale*, ignoring the thought
that it was now nearly midnight in Brisbane.

'Mother,' he said without preamble, 'I've
left Bosie.'

'Where, dear?' his mother asked. Her voice
came through as strongly as if she were in the
next phone booth.

'In Venice.'

'Darling,' Kathleen said, 'what a lovely place to leave her.'

Handing down the delicious Waterman into the gondola, that half version of a Melanesian war canoe, Brain was stabbed with *déjà vu*. Dad, he remembered. Mum. Two eccentrics he had regretted but delighted in as he matured. After his father's death mother had flung herself head first into evening courses and floundered through a bachelor degree in economics. Mother in her middle years on a borrowed bicycle, cycling all the way down the old Sandgate Road to attend a Corpus Christi procession at his college, cycling in her moth-eaten undergraduate gown, even though no one bothered wearing them those days, a trencher cockahoop on her skull, batwings flapping. It was his final year and he had tried pretending—oh shame! shame!—that he hadn't seen her as she propped her bicycle against the football oval fence and came seeking him out, grinning her excuse me's through the crowd and the roaringly sung *Pange Lingua*.

Mother! Oh Mother!

In guide-book Italian he asked the straw-boatered gondolier to take them up the canals to the railway station. There appeared to be some difficulty. The boatman kept shaking his head as Brain shouted '*Il stazione*' over the noise of police launches and ferries. Not even waved money bills of impossibly large denomination were lubricant. The gondolier poled away, taking huge and elegant sweeps with his oar, glancing occasionally at Mrs Waterman, who was too amused by the whole business to do more than catch that admiring Italian eye. After twenty minutes of graceful movement up and down the major canals they found themselves back where they had started.

'This is too much!' Brain cried, angered, and producing thousands of lire. The gondolier daringly kissed Mrs Waterman's fingertips, giving her ring finger the smallest of nips with his teeth, and refused to look at either of them

again as he waited for the next mad tourist. In
the end they were forced to take a water taxi.

Despite the spiritual dousing of the boatman who had tampered with spontaneity, there
they are, entrained, racing towards Milan and
points north of there. North to Zürich where
the Zürichsee would mirror its indifference to
their unadventurous adultery. Brain had been
expecting a sexual renaissance. Perhaps he was
in awe of his partner's almost phlegmatic
urbanity, despite the pneumatic attractions of
her pastel flesh. A sense of trespass which might
have sustained them failed to stimulate. Having
left all their possessions to be lugged about or
sent home by their abandoned partners, they
were forced to spend too much of their time
replenishing essentials. Exhausted and now irri-
tably guiltless, they tucked into *Sauerbraten* and
told each other how bored they had been in
their former lives. Bored, bored, bored, Nina
said, almost wolfing her tucker. Brain was
appalled by her healthy appetite.

They made no inquiries as to the reaction
of the tour party. They dismissed the anxiety —
if there were — of their spouses and pressed on
into Germany where they stayed for three days
in a hotel near the cathedral in Augsburg. On
the second morning as they left their hotel, Nina
expressed a most urgent need for chocolate and

they found themselves in an upstairs *Kaffeehaus* chockablock with huge German *Hausfrauen*, shelf-breasted like escritoires, demolishing mini chocolate mice and Dachshunds to muted Strauss. The air was trembling and breathing fur, perfume and the more subtle scent of overfeeding.

The waiter patronised their broken German and in perfect English pointed out errors of adjectival agreement and tense. At the next table an elderly sourpuss paused to absorb this half way through chomping, leaving a small nugget of mouse suspended by its candy tail from her gaping lips.

'Joyboy's mother,' Nina whispered, stricken unexpectedly by the antithesis between postwar gluttony and postwar horror. She smiled up at the waiter. 'Do you want me to explain? Do you remember "The Loved One"? The *dolce vita* is too ghastly.' She began shaking with silver ripples of laughter and then a noisy choking. 'Oh the death camps,' she said tactlessly to Brain. 'The ovens.'

Brain admonished through his own laughter.

Their hot chocolate was brought. Nina lowered her perfect profile to the cup and began sipping. Brain lit a cigarette and there were immediate cries of outrage from the table behind. The waiter returned from his on-guard position by the cash register and reprimanded him in excited German and then in English. Brain took one more drag on his cigarette before stubbing it out on his saucer, then he looked up and held the waiter's eye. Kathleen could have handled this, he thought, and said conversationally, 'Lots of smoke in Auschwitz. Why does one cigarette upset you?'

The waiter vanished and returned with the manager.

Residues of fifty-year-old resentments were all about them.

'I must ask you to leave immediately,' the manager said. He was a heavy man with fat-protected eyes of light blue.

Brain rose, holding out a hand to Nina. 'Nazi,' he suggested amiably. Somehow he didn't seem to care about anything any more.

They went down the stairs clutching laughter, anger and rails — the feeblest props.

Mrs Waterman told him he had been brave but foolish.

That's me, he thought, with the emphasis on *foolish*, and his fingers ran playful scales on the tender skin of her arm. He began humming as they walked to the Bahnhof, humming then singing softly under his breath, increasing the volume, a mobile busker, until at the station entrance, *plena voce*, he achieved a climax of farewell.

And the slow rain. The slow rain in Copenhagen, pitting sidewalks and window-sills, drowning hair and eyes in the slowest of tides, pocking the last snow in the parks.

Brain felt no urge to sing Tosti to parka-muffled Danes. He treacherously wondered if this haphazard union were part of the real thing. He wondered if she wondered as well, sitting on the edge of a lumpy bed in a second-rate hotel misnamed The Grand. They had sauntered through arcades, examined monuments and explored parks where the statues still wore neat singlets of snow. *Where was the bloody rapture?* Could he be, he wanted to know, self-embroiled in emotional swindle? He was startled to hear himself tell this near stranger—carnal partner that he ached to get back to the discomfort, the essential crudity of the homeland. The heat. The laissez-faire. Even, he added, allowing his lips to curl deprecatingly, the cockroaches. He especially missed them.

She took the wind out of his sails! What a dame! 'I miss them too.' Sentimentally rolling her lovely eyes. 'And I especially miss our own slack, mendacious brand of government. Easy come, easy take.'

The train run north had been more of a *via crucis* than a sentimental journey. They were pestered by another tourist who, recognising their accents, claimed kinship. The skinny lad announced that more than anything at all he wanted a lamb bloody chop. It seemed to sum up everything. Although Brain informed him that there were plenty where he was at present, the horrible traveller kept saying, 'Not like ours, mate. Not like ours.' Nina had whispered disloyally, 'Me too. I understand. I'm on his side. The short-loin side.' The youth, suspecting mockery, looked hard at them for the first time in an hour and translated their smiles. 'And sod you, too,' he said, moving away.

'Does that,' Brain asked, nodding after the denim back, 'still make you eager to return? Does it?'

'Of course,' she said.

The ferry crossing was delayed because of fog so thick nothing of the outer world was visible, a world choked with the cries of ships' bells and the mournful breves of sirens. During that rolling trip Nina suddenly clasped his hand saying, 'I have no wish to be difficult, my dear, but I feel I have reached the end. Terminus. I must get away, get back, as quickly as possible.' Then she closed her eyes and slept.

It was late when they had reached Copenhagen. Icy winds blew them momentarily apart as they came out of the station and headed across the square to the hotel. Mrs Waterman chose it because it was rumoured James Joyce had once stayed there. In the foyer a bellhop, determined on a tip, pressed so closely behind her as they waited to register she could hardly move. Baby fingers tangled with hers on the bag handle. She looked down and was surprised by the cold, pert determination of the fuzzless face. Carefully, meticulously, she raised each of the clutching fingers one after another, pressing them away, but as one finger was removed another would return with the persistence of an anemone. 'Go away, little boy!' she hissed. 'Away.'

The desk clerk raised his eyebrows.

Once in their room Brain offered the mildest of rebukes. 'That wasn't wise, dear.'

It was a ghastly room stinking of decay — old bodies, old clothing, damp towels. He began listing the mouldering objects.

'Humid prose.' Nina added.

'Whose what? What humid prose?'

'Joyce's for God's sake! Perhaps this was the very room.'

'What very room?'

'The room where Joyce . . . oh God, Brain, you're determined to madden. Nora Barnacle. Perhaps even . . . Oh never mind. I get the feeling they haven't touched a thing in here for years. National treasure at second-hand.'

He could not honestly tell her that she was his. He pulled off his shoes and socks and inspected his bare toes. The central heating was excessive. The window latches were stuck on decades of paint. There was a detumescent protestant stuffiness about the entire Scandinavian peninsula, despite affirmations of liberal sexual manners. Those too were overlaid with Lutheran censure.

Was he failing with her already?

There had been no discussion of future strategy. Former partners had been obliterated in unemotional whiteout, the word 'never' typed in. He had to force the next question, the salient word.

'Together? Us? You want to go back together?'

She wasn't stupid. She could assess. She crossed to the window and looked down at the sleet-filled landscape and the misty buildings.

Below on the sidewalk a group of walkers illuminated by the hotel entrance were skidding as they hurried against increasing snowfall. One of them fell flat on his back. She could interpret the 'O' of pain through the double glazing.

'For the moment, I suppose.' She turned and looked at him dubiously. 'There are other ways of partnering besides the bed.'

'What?'

'A business, perhaps. There must be something. Gallery? Craft shop? Cafe? A small but exquisite restaurant?'

The inner howling at memory of past failed business ventures surged up, escaped in a lewd moan in that dank room. He would have to do something, he supposed, but had not thought beyond the moment of freedom. If it were that.

She had moved away from the window and was busy brushing her hair, dragging the bristles through shining lengths as slowly as summer. Stroke after stroke.

Was she serious?

Sleepless on that lumpy bed in Copenhagen, Brain remembering through the sleet-filled night.

Two years ago another of his more exotic failures, for which he had, without a doubt, a kind of genius. Over the years there had been sharp exchanges with his brother-in-law, the minister for transports. Own up! He couldn't stand Len, couldn't bear his lamp-tanned ego-ridden confidence, the spanking way he hefted his cheapskate schemes through the barriers of local councils to make another financial killing.

Jealousy? Sure. Ferocious unabating envy.

Brain nosed around.

No wonder Sham and her husband were

rolling in the stuff. The Mercedes and the Porsche were hardly products of a backbencher's salary.

He nosed around.

He kept alert at parties.

He kept his ears open. Their antennae sensitively recorded the slightest frisson of shonky dealing. The wealth, he noted, had followed swiftly on electoral success. He was engaged by rumours of land deals up and down the coast and vast profits made from Japanese investors. Between his own misdirected concerns Brain conceived an ironic revenge whose jokiness might yet be turned to profit.

On a shaggy block of land on the highway north of Reeftown, a block he had purchased fifteen years before, he had begun erecting a three-storey . . . what? Humanoid? Pioneer figure? Tourist goggle-butt? The land was a poor few unserviced acres on the hillside above the sea, picked up cheap before the boom. Except when the bill for rates arrived each year, he had almost forgotten he owned it.

Come down in the world, Brain was working as evening bar manager at one of the glitzier resorts, a grocery-money job that gave him the days free. Bosie spent her mornings at the local golf club trying to achieve a hole in one. Connections who owed him a favour at a plastic and fibreglass mouldings factory became involved in his project, making mysterious sections without ever being aware of the total concept.

No one twigged.

Over three months of near-furtive activity, he trucked up huge anonymous pieces of bilda-kit and by the time legs, belly and chest were assembled, the monstrous torso was visible above the uncleared scrub on the fence line. Another week and he would be ready to lug the questing head up on ropes to drop onto its swivel axle so that Len's slack, tanned features could inspect the Coral Sea. North, south, north, south, to the whim of the trades, in the harbour, in the islands, he hummed, remembering his father and the singing in the Ascot evenings. His first political coup! Already busloads of tourists heading for the Port had noticed with excitement this mammoth artifact skulking behind acacia, and visitors in rented cars had been stopping to take photographs.

Wisely he slung a six-foot chain-wire fence across the frontage of his block and extended it partly up each side. He put a padlock on the swing gates. At the end of that week Len's conniving features were lowered into place by ropes and pulleys in early tropic darkness. Brain was so enraptured with the result he sat below his towering god savouring the proxy ecstasies of a pagan worshipper.

Within two days the council intervened.

'What the hell do you think you're doing?' the shire engineer asked. 'Did you apply for a permit? Anyway, what in God's name is it?'

Brain smiled modestly. He was choked with laughter. 'It's the Big Developer,' he said slyly. 'Related to the Big Cow, Prawn, Pineapple, Banana. It's a work of art. I don't have to apply for a development permit for a sculpture.'

The two of them stood in the shadow of thirty feet of moulded fibreglass and poured concrete, dodging the slab-like heat and humidity of mid-day. There was Len — hi, Len! — sporting natty tropical safari suit painted in semigloss acrylic, gold chain and white developer shoes. His legs, Brain pointed out to the unliterary shire engineer, bestrode the world like a Colossus. The tanned rubbery features and neurotic eyes moved on their swivel skull to the smallest breeze, gazing appetently up and down the coastline, seeking new empires.

'Smashing, isn't it!' Brain said. 'Unfortunately I've run out of money. I had intended a restaurant.'

'Restaurant?'

'Sure. Stairs up each leg, lavatories at the

flies—suitable, hey?—dining room at the
paunch and a revolving lookout in the skull.
Say cocktail bar, huh, where all the brain damage occurs. Nothing like a metaphor. It's a nice
idea, isn't it?'

'I think you're bloody mad,' the shire
engineer said. 'Get it down.'

'Hey, wait a minute,' Brain protested. 'It's
a statue. It's not a dwelling. It's not a restaurant. Not yet. There's nothing in the by-laws
about erecting a statue. It's beautification of my
land, mate.'

Rage transmuted the shire engineer's face
into a clone of the one swivelling above them.
Congested fury made him goggle. For a minute
Brain thought he was speaking faster than
sound.

'You'll hear more about this. There'll be a
council 'dozer up as soon as I can organise one.
That's if you don't get busy yourself. The thing's
caused traffic snarls, near accidents. Just look
down there now. Can't you see what it's doing?'
There were indeed five cars parked below on
the highway with excited families clambering
up the road margin. 'It's a bloody public hazard.'

He stumped off down the slope to his car,
now wedged between a bus and a truck. Japanese cameras clicked crazily as he approached.

Brain smiled. Already reporters had been

up to take shots and run stories in the local press. He liked to think of Shamrock's and Len's outrage when the Brisbane papers took it up. May they choke on their croissants! he hoped. He could hear the cough-splutter of tortured windpipes. It was a good likeness. Len could hardly fail to recognise his horrible self.

Brain grew high on wild sensations of pride. Flair, that's what it was. Flair.

His tragedy was a multiplicity of small talents.

'Hey!' Chaps said that week, on one of his brief visits home for money. 'Some kook has built a bloody great statue thing on the Cook Highway.'

'What of?' Bosie was waggling her finger-nails to dry them. She appeared to be clawing air.

'Well, it's a guy in a snappy safari suit. Looks like Uncle Len, actually.'

'Len?'

'Yeah. Got those bloodshot eyes. Shifty. You know how the Unk looks when you ask him anything. Guess it's a kind of libel. Doesn't look like a tribute.'

Attempting indifference his father asked carelessly, 'Did you go right up?'

'Couldn't get a park. There were two buses and half a dozen cars pulled in. I slowed right down, though. It's a gas!'

'My!' Brain laid down the paper and reached for the coffee pot, savouring the scent as he re-filled his cup, savouring the prospect of a relaxed afternoon by the pool. 'Causing a stir, is it? Maybe some civic-minded grateful member of Len's electorate decided it was time for public thanks.'

Chaps rubbed his freckles thoughtfully. 'It's certainly causing a stir. Everyone up in Port was talking about it. Maybe some hippy whacko freaked out.'

Bosie and Brain had been playing happy families: Mother, Bimbo and Chaps, all up for Mother's yearly visit. Bimbo had looked in only for a couple of nights on his way to Darwin. Chaps, who was leaving the next morning, could think only of that long run down the coast in a beat-up Holden that badly needed an overhaul. He judged, nicely gauging his father's pleased smirk about something or other, that it was time to put in the nips.

'What the hell do you do with your allowance? What about those casual jobs you're always telling us you've got?' Brain asked.

Bimbo and Chaps had only the blazer pockets of their Brisbane boarding school as

mementoes of five years' expensive education.
Bimbo had failed university political economy
and was thereby assured of administrative work
in a political party. 'Better if you hadn't done
any of that crap,' the party secretary told him.
'Spoils your judgement. Still, we'll give you a
go. Temporary.' The wily lad had only recently
decided to throw in his genius with the national
coalition. Uncle Len had applied some pressure
but not, Bimbo thought resentfully, nearly
enough. 'Why them?' his father asked. 'More
perks,' Bimbo explained briefly as he gazed
critically around his parents' outdoor living room
where, my God, those old sixties carbuncular
speakers were still playing forties big band
muck! Still, he'd be gone soon. His olds bored
him rigid. Bosie was a complete turbo mouth
once she got going. He wondered how the old
man stood it and for the shortest of moments
(to be calculated in microseconds) he patted his
father's sad, greying thatch and regarded the
poor wrinkled neck with compassion. That vul-
nerable nape! Instinctively he rubbed his own,
dreading. Chaps wasn't nearly as critical—yet.
He was still into eating and muscle-building
and lapped the pool endlessly, his shoulders
darkened by sun, glistening with oil, stroking
away in brilliant chlorinated waters.

Woooosh!

But you were the oddball, Daisy said, *weren't you?*

Kathleen found her thoughts inevitably meshed with those of her son and his crackpot stratagems. *Both of us*, she answered.

The hypnotic quality of sun burning slant-wise through the mall and the whoop of traffic in side streets kept trying to extinguish that last Christmas with its sour hostess and the guttering candles of a failed marriage. *You don't want to hear all this stuff*, she said to Daisy, who refused to stay in that seat opposite, who kept getting up and moving away. *The more I remember the more I'm loaded with this sense of responsibility, the conviction that somewhere along the line I went horribly wrong.*

But you kept moving, didn't you? Daisy asked. *Spiritually, I mean. You don't even have to leave your chair for that.*

I know that, Kathleen said impatiently. *God, I know that! How would I ever have managed, for goodness' sake! How would you? Listen. How about this for zany? You want zany, I'll give you zany!*

A pilgrimage.

'But this is your land!' Bosie had accused shrilly as the three of them panted up the scrubby slope in the late afternoon to what Brain insisted on calling his *coup de vie*. 'Oh Brain, how could you do this to Len?'

She had insisted on being shown. His mother had come for laughs.

'Easy.'

'No wonder the council . . .'

'Trespass. Trespass if they touch one plastic hair of his head.'

'Bullshit!' his wife screamed, forgetting her refinement. 'Bullshit, Brain! I don't know how you could do this.'

Then he told her how he could with such
detail she started screeching about family dis-
loyalty, thoughtlessness, producing a litany of
damage that might affect the boys quite apart
from the offensiveness to someone as pleasant,
as clever, as obliging . . .

'You've forgotten rich,' he said. 'And slimy
bastard.'

His mother was overcome with unsuitable
mirth. 'I love it,' she kept croaking. 'Absolutely
love it. The ultimate garden gnome.'

'Of Zürich,' her son added. 'There were
rumours and rumours, probably all with
foundation.'

Bosie was staring at her gaga mother-in-
law with loathing. She was outraged by Kathleen's response, even if the old girl wasn't all
there. God! Shrillings of 'laughing-stock', 'libel
actions', 'public fools' leapt easily from her lips.
And in truth when they tottered down to the
road there was a knot of photographers and
reporters to meet them. Mother, Brain observed,
could not subdue the joyous tug of her mouth.

Yes, Brain admitted to the cub reporter
from the *Reeftown Herald*, oh yes, it was most
certainly his land. Would she care for the title
deed number? And certainly he was aware that
the . . . er . . . statue was there. Had he built
it? he was asked. Cameras buzzed like cicadas.

He was not prepared to answer that question at this stage. Did he know who had built it? they persisted. He reminded them of the respected journalist tradition of never revealing one's source. There were unbelieving smiles.

'He did!' his Judas wife shrieked at the end of her loyal tether. 'He built the bloody thing!'

'Is that so?' one of the reporters asked. He winked at Brain.

The cameraman took a lot of snaps of Bosie with mouth agape and teeth flashing. She would hate herself the next day.

'No.' Brain lied with the assurance of a politician, with that same meretricious ease. Momentarily he wondered if his talents perhaps lay in government. 'It certainly is not so. I simply made my land available. It's a statement.'

'Of what?'

'I'm afraid I will have to leave you to make your own assumptions.'

'Are you going to pull it down, Mr Hackendorf?'

'I'm not going to.'

'Do you think the council will?'

'They might try. They might trespass. I'm taking legal advice.'

For the moment the only advice he had taken was that of Nina Waterman, whom he

had driven there for a viewing before the head
was mounted. An afficionada of galleries and the
dubiousness of gallery-speak, she had brought
the trimmings for al fresco lunching — champagne and ice-bucket, flamboyant qualifiers to
the outing where they had clinked champagne
flutes over the grass-snuggling features of
Brain's brother-in-law. Mrs Waterman, who
rarely yielded to emotional admission, rocked
with laughter as she christened the head, then
seated herself firmly on a nearby log artistically
lugged beneath a recently planted grove of fan
palms. From below on the highway came the
screech of cars braking and excited chatter in a
variety of languages.

'So what do you think?'

'Marvellous!' Champagne slopped onto the
grass. 'Absolutely marvellous! Who did you say
the gentleman is?' She leant forward and poured
a little more wine over Len's snuggling features.

'My brother-in-law,' Brain said with ap-
propriate modesty. 'The minister for transports.'

'Whose? Whose transports?'

'Originally my sister's, one hopes. Now,
who knows?'

Mrs Waterman rolled these shreds of fact
around and hogged more champagne. 'Delicious, my dear. Oh delicious.'

Yet after the newspaper assaults, Brain

proceeded with a legal ban on council intrusion and somehow his lawyer managed to slap an injunction on proceedings. For another fort-night buses continued to pull up. From the seaward side of the highway visual access to the upper torso was rendered easier by a mound of granite boulders flung up by some geologi-cal spasm on which camera-wielding tourists perched like excited gulls. In Brisbane the min-ister for transports contemplated suing but decided, pushed by Shamrock, on a public and dignified silence and a private donation to Reef-town's council funds. He gave one television interview only, on which the bastards kept moving between his features and those of his fibreglass twin, and sat back and waited.

During that period, in a last satiric lunge, Brain erected a large sign, THE BIG DEVEL-OPER, near the gates and cleared scrub all round for twenty yards each way so that the belly and legs were visible from the road.

The shire engineer retreated behind a maze of legal paperwork.

Dispensing with thoughts of foxhole, re-doubt, stockade, barbette, circumvallation or even a primitive abatis for protection, Brain took to sleeping on the block after he had left work at the bar, huddled in a pup tent pitched beneath the statue's straddling legs. Why, old

Len, he thought sourly, sweating in his sleeping bag, two vast and trunkless legs of stone.

Four nights later, when Brain drove up after midnight had belched into silence at the Jungle Bar, he found that during the day the council, someone, had settled the matter. The chainwire fence had been flattened for ingress and the Big Developer exploded into fragments that lay all over the grove. His pup tent hung raggedly from the lower branches of a wattle.

Fury. Despair. Then laughter. Rational about it, he knew he had had his moment and was sated, more or less, when next morning's *Reeftown Herald* ran the following report:

> *A mysterious explosion last night was heard clearly by residents of Casuarina Beach and as far away as the Port.*
>
> *It appears to have been located at the site of what has come to be known as The Big Developer, a 10-metre statue erected on the freehold property of a well-known local identity, Mr Brian Hackendorf.*
>
> *Local feelings are mixed about the destruction of what some called a monstrosity and others a witty and authentic tourist attraction.*
>
> *Whatever the outcome, we can be sure that a certain southern politician is relieved.*

*When asked for comment the Reeftown Shire
Council, who had strongly opposed the project,
refused to make a statement.*

Brain smiled and sighed. Bosie's smirk scorched.
    Another failure?
    Success?

Hey, Daisy, Daise! Kathleen had said over the
chocolate cake that day, *there's more to it. Much
more. I've skipped the grandma years. Think I'll write
a book about those. Funny Doctor Spock never thought
of it. Could have made another million. The guide
to grandmothering. The four ages of women: Bimbo,
breeder, baby-sitter, burden.* Daisy had slopped tea
all over her cake plate. *Need someone to baby-sit*

me, she said. *I'm at the burden stage myself.* She had crooked a mock-elegant finger and asked about the four ages of man. Which one of them had said *Hunk, hunk, hunk, hunk?* She couldn't remember anything except the splatterings of mirth.

There's a limit, Kathleen decided, angry too late, to the amount of work families can squeeze from the withering muscles of grandmothers.

Over the years she had become accustomed to her daughter's voice, hardened by distance. Mother — the wires refused to dimple — can you take Bridgie for me next weekend? Len has to attend a conference in Melbourne, Sydney, Perth, Hobart . . . Her job spared her week-day trials and her son's removal to the far north much more. But the baby years of Bimbo and Chaps had eaten into her own free time week after week. When Shamrock gave birth to Bridgie she had just taken early retirement. Am I unnatural, she wondered, lying vigorously to avoid a long weekend at her daughter's home, a weekend of yowls and laundry while Shamrock and Len lived it up at a ritzy hotel in Melbourne. They think, she thought sourly, I can't wait to get my hands on this grandchild, that I'm bereft of hugs, kisses, cuddle-time. They've got to be crazy!

Beyond all that now, she plucked up the nagging phone and held it away from her ear, pulling a face at the hot Brisbane street outside. Cars were terrorising an old man trying to cross the pedestrian walkway. They kept speeding through while he fluttered his frail bones on the lip of the footpath.

'I'm terribly sorry,' she lied, 'but I'm going to Tamborine for that week. It's all booked.'

'Couldn't you take Bridgie with you?'

'Couldn't you? It's not as if she's at the toddler stage. In fact Bridgie and I have more in common than you think. We've both reached the burden period of our lives.'

'Oh God, Mother. She'd be bored witless. Come on, I don't ask that much of you.'

'Not these days, no. But still no.'

'What do you mean, no? Heavens, you're unnatural. You are her grandmother after all. Most grandmothers are panting to do a little something.'

'Not this grandmother,' Kathleen said. 'I am no longer panting. I've done my fair share of that.' She watched two cars play chicken with each other around the old man, who had now ventured ten paces out onto the roadway. The cars vanished in screaming exhaust fumes towards the river. 'In fact, more than my fair share.'

'But look, it's not as if Bridgie is a baby

any more. She's thirteen, for God's sake, and
perfectly capable of entertaining herself. It's ages
since I asked you. All of five weeks.'

'No, dear. Sorry. I'm five weeks weaker.
Can't she stay over with one of her school
friends? Why can't she go with you if she's perfectly capable of entertaining herself?'

Kathleen envisaged Sham's stubborn bottom lip thrust out with resentment. Already
Bridgie was smoking, boy-mad, and given to
sneaked swigs of alcohol. She was expensive to
run. She had been expelled from two private
schools and was having disciplinary problems in
her third.

The line hummed with incommunication.

'Look, Mother, this is really the last time
I'll ask you, I promise. Len wants me to go with
him as a kind of personal trip.'

Kathleen remembered unremembered
birthdays, her often lonely Christmases, the
presents unthanked, casually treated.

'Does he, darling?'

'Yes, he does.'

'Well, I'm sorry,' she said, 'but it's still no.'

Sham slammed the phone into its cradle
at the precise moment the old man reached the
far side of the road and collapsed. Kathleen saw
two pensioners tottering to assist, picked up the
morning paper and read:

*An elderly woman found wandering in a late
night supermarket at Chermside was unable to
tell police what she was doing or even where she
lived. Police investigating discovered that she had
an interstate bus ticket from Newcastle but no
means of identification. The woman was unable
to tell them her name or address, although she
was under the impression that her daughter had
purchased the ticket.*

    Inquiries are proceeding.

To proceed: Sham instantly found a compliant
doctor who booked her into a private clinic for
observation. She had developed mysterious and
strangling cramps in her lower abdomen. The
hospital rang Kathleen as next of kin. Within
an hour of the phone call Bridgie arrived on
her grandmother's doorstep, lightly swinging a
beach bag, a pack, jean-stuffed, drooping over
her shoulder. She wore too much eye makeup
and her jaws worked busily at gum.

'Hi,' she greeted the open door. Then
she pushed rudely past her grandmother and
dumped both bags in the hallway.

'Shouldn't you be at school?'

'Pupil-free day,' Bridgie said without interest. 'We get loads of them.'

'Now wait a minute, Bridgie,' Kathleen
protested. 'What is this? What's going on?'

Bridgie ignored the question. 'Gotta sit.'

She sprawled immodestly on the living-room sofa.

'Answer me,' Kathleen demanded. 'I said what's going on?'

Bridgie looked up and grinned around gum. She explained languidly with limp finger movements. Mother had been rushed to a clinic right on lunchtime. Bridgie was undisturbed by the news she delivered. She dragged herself up from the sofa, ambled out of the living room and began raiding the refrigerator for juice. Kathleen could hear the crashes of shoved-aside dishes coming from the kitchen. Tracking the noise spoor!

She went out to the kitchen herself. 'I'm beginning to understand,' she said testily, 'why they killed the messenger. Bridgie, tell me immediately what is going on. I don't understand.'

'God, Grandma, don't you?'

Bridgie was an aggressively pretty child who used insolence as a cosmetic aid. She did raised eyebrows and wrinkled nose. She gulped the last of Kathleen's orange juice.

'It's a ploy. She isn't really sick, not sick sick. She'll be right by the weekend, just in time for Daddy's Perth junket. She suspects he's on with one of the secretaries, actually.' Bridgie looked down at the dregs of flavoured mineral water in her glass. 'Pure puke, Grans.'

'You didn't have to drink it,' Kathleen

rejoined vigorously. She removed the emptied bottle and rammed it in the waste bin, a task that seemed not to engage her grandchild's consciousness, while she repressed cosseting memories of a tear-stained four-year-old Bridgie displaying grazed knees and wet pants. What possible relationship did that mucus-streaked baby face sodden with tears bear to this teen-age pouter brilliant with gold glitter and lip gloss?

Bridgie rolled her eyes in a world-weary fashion.

'Mother told me to come here.'

'Well, mother was wrong. I'm going away this afternoon for a little holiday. It's paid for and I'm not cancelling now simply to please your mother's suspicious whims. You can go back at once. I'll ring for a cab.'

'But there's no one at home.' Bridgie allowed a badly-done-by whine to creep into her voice.

'Now Bridgie, that won't really worry you one little bit, will it? In fact, knowing your record, darling, you'd prefer it.'

A sly smile flickered on Bridgie's lips.

'And I've no money.'

'My shout,' Kathleen said. She watched Bridgie's eyelids blink, concealing a brazen blaze.

'Okay, Grans.' Kathleen could tell she was
doing mental arithmetic at computer rates as
she calculated blackmail. The child stifled a
yawn.

'That's a good girl. I'll get the cab to take
you to your mother's clinic first. She can sort it
out from there. Do you know the address?'

'Sure. She's often used it. She flogs Daddy
with it. It's her panic hole. It's very expensive.'

Quite suddenly the two of them were
smiling at each other.

'You're not really going away, are you,
Grans?' Bridgie asked complacently.

Kathleen said, 'I decline to answer that
question on the grounds that it might incrimi-
nate me. You know, Bridgie, sometimes you
make me feel quite young.'

'Hey,' the kid said, 'that's great! That's
really great! You know, Grans, I really like you.
This should stuff it up for both of them.'

Could it have been that barely recalled firming
of the spirits three years ago that now found
her Lear-like between the homes of son and
daughter, who had dutifully but reluctantly

offered haven and then made living in that
haven impossible? The patterned landscape of
her past had altered with the scumbling effects
of time, presenting this day, this week, this year,
as the blurred and entrancingly beautiful proto-
plast of an unskilled impressionist — as if she
herself had cunningly but deliberately smudged
the still-wet shapes and outlines.

Programmed, of course, to accept the
blame.

Were you a scapegoat, too? she had asked
Daisy, Daisy's mouth smudged with cream and
her own fogged past.

Whatever had Daisy replied? Her memory
going while she lived in a world of names that
more and more frequently refused to attach
themselves immediately to the right object, any
old word tumbling off the tongue, come trip-
pingly, oh she could recall the Elizabethans, but
only fragments of this hot present continuous
in Brisbane town where even the town's silhou-
ette was so changed from that of youthful recall
it was as if she were living somewhere else. And
the impatience that greeted that loss! The irri-
tability and the mouth-munching as she fought
for a place, a person! Yet across that stretched
canvas, when she tried not to remember, names
and incidents stuck with the particularity of
rocks in a reef. There was no searching, no

fumbling. The days laid themselves out, laid themselves out, in the sequential design of a cunningly constructed game of chess.

End game?

Hers?

But where for the restart, the new beginning?

Reeftown, Brain realised, was replete with the memory of failures. There were the unshed spouses as well. Not of course that Reeftown society raised its eyebrows at marital peccadilloes. From the town's beginnings, from the pitching of tents on the banks of a river that snaked its way across the tablelands to drop a thousand feet before wandering through what had once been swamp and mangrove to the sea, a tolerance to irregularities in wedlock prevailed. The mosquitoes had always made concentration difficult.

Yet Reeftown was the world in a way. A paraphrase of the microcosm. A précis. On the eyelid rim of sleep they had mumbled about where, the inevitable *ubi* of lifetimes that ultimately ten thousand years from now—or even fifty—would mean nothing.

Not there, Nina had yawned sleepily, wiping from her mind the possibilities of that palm- and tourist-infested town that had fed her mind-blood for so long. *But* of *there*. She could never escape the northern tug, never erase. He had shaken her into wakefulness to demand exactly what she meant by those throwaway words and she answered that they were certainly not that. She fell asleep at last but in the morning, with grey snowlight between the long grubby drapes, she described the next town south, with its ugly gobbet of rock staring across five miles of aquamarine to an island that tugged.

'But not *on* the island.'

She watched Brain's eyes, red-veined from insomnia. 'Not on. Somewhere along the coast on the escarpment. Just north or south.'

They left the hotel, searching for a breakfast bar. He drew a mud map for her in the slush of Copenhagen as they stood near a *pølse* vendor's stall. They planned their restaurant with tomato sauce from the hot sausage running down their fingers. Everything seemed fine then. It was easier not to think.

As now, Brain thought, momentarily imagining Bosie in a nimbus of humiliated rage, cleaning out his belongings back in Reeftown. He envisaged her shredding the sheet music, raping the tape deck, hauling down the speakers by the pool. All she would be left with, he reflected bitterly, was the house she stood up in, a million-dollar ocean-front and an annuity from her developer daddy.

Nina and he had returned in almost inelegant haste from Europe for a fortnight of spouse acrimony. Well, his, in fact. Mr Waterman, Nina told him, was totally absorbed in his collection of postcards, grabbed between bouts of diarrhoea at tourist spots throughout Europe and the United Kingdom, and had become obsessed with one particular brown reproduction of the classroom at Hawkshead Grammar. He kept wondering, though he put it more delicately, if Wordsworth had really bonked his sister.

'I'm moving out,' Nina announced.

'Are you dear?'

'Charles, you're not listening. You never listen.'

'Yes I am. I do. But look, Nina, I have his

collected letters. I have infinite comments made by his contemporaries. And after all he did have that little fling in France which must, don't you agree, have acted as some kind of ultimate moral slackening — if indeed, it weren't a warner! — wouldn't you think? Such a philosophic-stroke-pantheist Christian, if I can put it that way. One boggles.'

'You can put it any damn way you like, the emphasis being stroke. Do you mind if I take the clock radio?'

'Not at all. Take whatever you want, my dear. Yet there is something suspect. Oh I don't know. It's the disease of post-Freudians, isn't it, to attribute sexual appetence to almost everything.'

'And what about the tapes? Fifty fifty? Half and half?'

'My dear, whatever. Look at the whole thing this way: here's William; here's Dorothy. Now . . .'

But Nina had already left the room and was ramming clothes into cardboard boxes. When she emerged to ring for a taxi, her husband was still brooding over a blow-up of Wordsworth's cottage.

'On second thoughts,' she said, 'I won't take the radio.'

'Won't you, dear?'

'No.'

'Or the tape deck?'

There was a rude hooting from outside under the tulip trees.

'That's it,' she said. 'Goodbye, Charles. Look after yourself.' He looked up as she lugged cases and boxes towards the door.

'You too, dear. Where are you off to now?'

She became furious. The honking outside repeated its primitive motif. Charles had easily won that round. Or was he even trying? That was the rub, that probably he was not even aware.

'I'm not sure,' she replied, allowing the cold and the heat to bite through her words. 'I'll be in touch.'

'Of course,' he said.

Of course, of course, of course.

So there they were at last, the two adulterers, perched, re-plumaged parrots, on a ridge-roost of the Great Divide, too far (couldn't you guess?) from tourist traffic to make a financial killing, yet so awkwardly angled to tourism that the low-priced leasehold, the almost negligible rates, were constants in their conversations on profit and loss. But those, Brain realised in his growing disillusion, suspecting she did also, were nothing to do with the dwindling spiritual gains, the unrelenting mathematics of their own relationship.

The restaurant was a kind of shed-like

structure, all veranda and air, tarted with bamboo artifacts and tapa cloth. It had failed two previous owners. A short distance uphill was a small dwelling with small hot bedrooms and kitchen for the cafe management.

'But the pluses!' Nina was in the first flush of proprietorship. The restaurant verandas gaped at a coastal plain that paused with astonishment before prairies of swinging blue. Bluer than blue. The staggering brilliance of still unsullied waters. 'Just look at that . . . that dayspring!' Islands sailed untroubled along the marge, as indifferent as ships. Her partner, however, was gazing peevishly at the road in, a rutted memory of bitumen sustaining it, and a gradient that would attract only the most dedicated gastronome.

'The cooking,' he commented, 'will have to be bloody good to get customers tackling that track.'

'We'll need a staff of at least four,' Nina said dreamily. 'A superb chef, for a start.'

'But I thought—'

'I see myself rather as hostess of the cash register. Gracious troubleshooter. You, my dear, will be excellent in the bar.'

Will I indeed! Oh the souring of fact.

The longer they spent on primitive addition and the frightening aspect of overdrafts,

the more their enthusiasm was buffeted. It was
difficult, despite widespread unemployment, to
find staff. The pair of them were forced back on
their own efforts and Nina, in the early evening
as they waited hopefully for the trickle of diners
who had begun to face the distance and the
horror of the road up the ridge, would put on a
tape of Italian lusciousness and sing along with
tenors about Napoli and Sorrento, snapping her
fingers and thumbs during the fast bits and
swinging her hips to the insidious rhythms. She
was still a woman of voluptuous dimensions,
her face moulded on harmonious bones protected by the lushest of camellia flesh. Despite
the languor of weather, her hips swung vigorously between checking things in the kitchen,
whipping up a sauce or altering a table setting.
She cha-cha'd vocally with tenors of renown.

Business was slow.

It seemed never to stop, this mediterra-
nean mode. *Ai yi!* carolled sumptuous Nina,
jittering along with the Gipsy Kings, who
sounded as if they had missed the last train to
Madrid and were determined everyone would
suffer. *Ai yi!* she cried as diners straggled in. *Ai
yi yi!* With small heel stampings, arms curved
above heavenly head, fingers clicking. Brain
wondered if she were having a breakdown and
patted her with lingering hand on his way to

mix highballs and uncork wine with spurious flourish. Yet later, the diners vanished in puffballs of dust on the hill road, he would yield to her taste for the saccharine and sing once more *M'han detto che domani, Nina vi fate sposa*, even though his eyes caught a tiring light on the edge of hers.

'Does it matter?' she would ask in the sensual mornings, moisture still dripping from gutter and leaf, sunlight carving through green. She would roll, lazily naked under the sheets that were still too hot and heavy to bear.

'What? Does what matter?'

Sometimes he thought disloyally that since leaving Bosie he had merely changed guards.

'The money, my dear, the money.'

'What money? We're not making any. My overdraft is strangling me. This is game-playing, isn't it? It really is.' He was afraid to gouge out the truth of the matter: that each of them had used the other as an excuse for shedding a worn-out relationship. He cursed those fallaciously greener distant hills!

Nina flung her portion of sheet pettishly across his and stalked naked to the bathroom. Water would restore.

But it restored nothing beyond a temporary freshness of skin that lasted minutes only and the days, weeks, months, developed their own patterns of boredom and predictability as each secretly began wondering about their former partners and the flattened curves of their life-styles. Nina began gallery hopping again. Brain resumed golf. Their flight from responsibility rewarded them inversely for the gallery crowd took up their restaurant as an out-of-town dining quirk and golf club acquaintances picked up in the club bar began eating there on Saturday nights. A bit of a buzz, really, they told each other, to drive fifty miles for nosh up one of the worst back roads on the coast. Still, that dame of his was definitely something else and by the second bottle of Dom Perignon it all seemed worth it. The food wasn't too bad at all, they convinced themselves, if you liked pictures of food on plates. That *nouvelle cuisine*!

Once or twice Nina's extrovert welcomes made strangers wonder if she went with the coffee. Scatty Brain refused to be amused.

Could their renaissance in this gimcrack Eden last?

They feared asking each other in the perfection of those dud, those imperfect days.

Mother had rung.

Mother had rung from Brisbane.

Bad news comes in half-heard spurts on faulty lines, in blotched faxes, in hysteric mouthings impotent to control the outpourings of disaster.

Her house, she had told him, was being resumed for an expressway. Yes, of course she had known. For years, actually, but knowing government departments, had believed it would never happen. How long? The last five years. Well? Well, she had a month to move.

How could he explain without the corollaries of pain-giving, of rejection, that they had only just begun their business, that things were dicey? Over eight hundred miles of rustling and trembling wire he recognised her recognising rejection. *What about Sham?* he had asked brightly, hoping for respite. The silence became one of those cartoon balloons designated to be filled in with suitable captions. He couldn't think of any. *Well, yes, okay*, he agreed to the unspoken exegesis. *She's a pretty busy lady, I guess.* (Lady! Sham! . . . Jesus! Married to that slack-mouth whose limpness of feature measured his limpness of political purpose yet who managed, despite obvious defects like a low intelligence quotient, a dependence on liquor and a fluid expense account, to con his electorate every few years into returning him to the perks of office! Len had even escaped from the Heart of Darkness with minimal losses in his bank account. Wherever that was! No resting place for an outspoken woman like mother, who was now forgetting what she wanted to be outspoken about. Who forgot to pay bills or paid twice. Who missed bus, train, plane connections and stopped mid-sentence and asked, her tired eyes baffled and pained by the memory lapse, 'Now what was I saying, Brain? I've totally forgotten.')

'The Croziers,' he would prompt. 'You were telling me about the Croziers.'

'Who are they?'

'The people you went to visit . . . oh never mind.'

'Oh.' He could feel distant mother tense

as she struggled with the name. 'No dear. I think you've got it wrong. I can't remember anyone of that name.' Half an hour later, he knew, it would all rush in, drowning, a deluge of memories but twenty years earlier. She would probably ring back. 'Oh Brain, those Croziers. The ones who . . .' And off she would rattle on a nostalgia binge the edges of which he could barely recall himself.

Now, oh now, he yielded.

'Do you want to come up, Mum? For a visit? Just till you get things sorted?'

'Could I, dear? Not for long, I promise. Remember old Sam whosit, after three days guests and fish stink. I think that's what he said.'

'Johnson. Sam Johnson. He said that.'

'Did he? Well, he was so right. Probably something to do with his skin problem. Hard being a host with skin problems. Sham always makes me feel I have scrofula before I even arrive, to say nothing of that dreadful husband of hers.'

'The minister for transports!' Brain chuckled.

'Who else?' He could hear his mother's answering laugh.

They fixed dates, times. Nina said of course. She had liked Brain's zany old wool-gatherer of a mother the moment they met.

When was it—two, three years ago at one of those Christmas bashes Bosie insisted on having. Why, she might even help out, in the least tiring way, of course, on the busy nights, if ever there were busy nights. Did Brain think she would mind?

Brain had shaken his head. Of course she wouldn't mind. He was beginning to understand at last the healing quality of being needed, just at that point, though he didn't realise that, when his mother was tiring of being used.

He sighed now and looked at his watch.

His mother's plane was due in an hour and shortly he would drive down the zigzag track to the coast plains and head south for the airport, dumped between the constant sea and the constant hills.

The police had run Kathleen to earth in a small motel in Buderim. She was tackling her second breakfast egg. They were very kind to her, rang her daughter and checked to see the old girl had been picked up later that morning.

Shamrock was ferocious at having to drive all that way to collect (she made it sound like a parcel in her recriminations), having booked her mother on the tour out of kindness. Len received concessions on most of those things.

'Why did you do it?'

When the tour bus had stopped for a morning-tea break, mother had wandered off and hidden in a shopping mall, emerging only when she thought the rest of the party might have moved on. The bus captain, bedevilled by timetables, had reported one missing passenger to the local police and driven the other pensioners off along the coast.

'They were boring old farts,' Kathleen said.

She seemed unaware that she had done anything amiss.

Now Brain, hanging around the airport terminal, sweating charity, dread and love, recalled another phone call barely a month ago, coming mid-evening as he and Nina had been wrestling with a pudding course for three picky diners. His mother's voice was barely audible. He had asked her where she was calling from. She told him she didn't know. What city? he had inquired with heavy irony. She was testy when she said it was somewhere in Brisbane, New Farm way she thought, having strolled into the park, dozed on a seat by the river and absent-mindedly wandered out the wrong end. 'I'm not sure how to get home,' she said.

'There don't seem to be any buses and I don't want to walk back through the park in the dark. All the shops round here are closed.' 'For Chrissake!' Brain had screamed. 'Why me? Why don't you ring Sham?' She complained that her daughter got too angry. He suggested she ring a cab. There was no phone book, she told him. She was lucky there was a handset. Stay in the call-box, he instructed her. Don't move. He would fix something. He seemed to be on the phone for hours. The pudding was ruined.

The police were pleasant that time, too, and drove Kathleen right home, seeing her to the very door.

Was she more difficult than vague? Was that it? Sometimes, he had to concede, she was sharp as a tack. As far as he knew she coped with being alone, still managed with reading, the garden, getting to the shops. He didn't want to admit she needed companionship, fought that admission when that was the one thing, he was beginning to realise, he could possibly do without.

A small history of forgetfulness started. She was locked after hours in a gallery, a cemetery, two large city stores, and overslept in several cinemas. 'She talks to herself a lot,' Sham had replied to his concerned phone calls. 'I've heard her out in the yard admonishing plants. God, Brain, I can't handle it.'

Beaten. He was forced to yield.

'She's bloody lonely,' he said. 'You could do something about that.'

'So could you,' snapped his sister tartly.

Part Three

*I*nvestigations are still under way to discover the identity of an elderly couple found seated late last night in the departure lounge of a Sydney domestic air terminal.

Police were alerted by staff long after all local flights had ceased.

Both people, who are estimated to be in their late seventies or early eighties, appeared dazed and incoherent. They had no identification on them and medical reports indicate each is suffering from Alzheimer's disease. The woman, who is slightly more lucid than the man assumed to be her husband, insisted they were waiting for the return of their daughter who had gone to check luggage.

At present they are being looked after in temporary hostel care.

Anyone who can identify the couple from the above photograph is asked to contact Sydney metropolitan police.

Sydney Star, *15 December 1990*

*I*T WAS A NEW SOULSCAPE, this once-familiar home town with its highrise hotels and plethora of shopping ritz. But the rock remained immutable, its ugliness and scarred eastern face racing her so fast into the past, she felt choked for air, still standing on those lower slopes where once the traveller in electrical goods had kissed her stupid.

They drove by former landmarks—her childhood home, the rented house on Stanton

Hill with Ronald gloomily surveying the coast. Flinders Street had been transformed into a lengthy walking mall of trees and cafes, the esplanade a relentless string of motels. It was only when the car moved north from town, threading back-streets to the highway, past still-remembered gardens and verandas hiding behind mango trees, that she became aware they were actually leaving those lost, secret but open places of her youth.

'I'd somehow thought,' she ventured, her eyes stuck fast on slipping scenery, 'that the island . . . that you . . .'

Brain sighed. 'But I told you. I did tell you. We decided against that. I'm running you north. Not too far. We're up in the hills. You'll like that.'

But even after they had reached the restaurant and its tiny cottage and Nina had welcomed and helped her unpack and she had been settled on the lounger on the veranda with a cool drink, Kathleen persisted. *Why now? Why never before?*

'I've been wanting,' she said, 'to go there. I really thought that was where you were, you know. Sentimental rubbish, I suppose.'

'But which island?' Brain couldn't resist asking.

'The first. One's first island is very like . . .'

'Like what?'

Kathleen began humming. 'I've forgotten, my dear,' she said cunningly.

But she wouldn't let go of it. As if compelled she worried the matter over the next few days. 'I must go,' she kept saying as she lay back under the flickering patterns of the vine screens, her eyes drifting beyond to the almost indistinguishable line between sea and sky, teasing her into awareness of the almost but never quite forgotten things that prowled the margins of memory. It was as if some membrane between here and there and now and then were ruptured by the keenness of time's edge. 'I'll have to go back.' She wasn't aware she had said it aloud.

'It's all changed,' Brain insisted. He swirled his glass and listened to the ice cubes crack. 'You won't find it the same place at all.'

'But the old pub? Where your father and I?'

'Gone. Blew down in a cyclone twenty years back.'

'You mean there's nothing there? I'd still like to see.'

'There's too much there,' he said, brutal with her wistfulness. 'One of these days,' he had promised, 'we'll take a run over. Lots of houses now. Motels. Pools. Shops. I don't think you'll recognise it, Mum.'

You don't know about islands, Ronald had

accused on the hot sands of the little bay.

Oh I know now, she explained to her son and Daisy and maybe Ronald. They enclose, they are their own world.

'Ah well,' she said to Brain. And took his words for their smooth surface. 'It'd be nice if I had Daisy with me.'

'Daisy?'

'I've told you about Daisy.'

'So you have.' Brain had brought his drink out to the veranda and settled beside her. 'Good old Daisy. What happened to her?'

Kathleen refused to answer. *She's still around*, she whispered.

She kept staring over at the sea, peering for the humped shadow of the island, knowing it there and drawn towards rediscovery.

'Why all the brooches, Daisy?' she had asked.

Daisy had poured herself another cup of tea before answering. 'The kids. Each time the kids were born he gave me a brooch.'

'But Daisy, you only had six kids.'

'So?'

'You're wearing seven. What's the seventh?'

She had given a sly smile, old Daisy, and an almost forgotten pink crept over the wrinkled cheeks. Kathleen looked at the cheap collection of trinkets pinned to Daisy's summer floral. 'Mother' brooches, junk blue and red bits of glass surrounded by yellowing curlicues of metal. High on her shoulder sat a single pearl on a silver bar.

'That's a nice one. When did he give you that?'

Daisy grinned her old cheeky smile that rejuvenated the worn face, the thinning thatch. 'That wasn't him, Kath. That was a lugger man from up the Gulf, down in Charco for a breather. Cost me a broken nose, that did, and a couple of blackened eyes. But I kept it, despite the old bastard. Hid it and only brought it out when he was away on runs. Wonder what happened to him, old lugger-bugger I mean. Jimmy. That was his name. Wanted me to run away with him, but how could I with all those kids, eh?'

How could she?

Poor Daisy! It seemed that if she weren't in hospital giving birth, she was back there with broken ribs, snapped wrist, suspected concussion. Despite the brooches.

'Oh Daisy!' Kathleen had wanted to cry.

Daisy reached across for another cream bun.

'Dropped dead in the bar of the Sovereign not long after Bibby, she's the sixth.'

'But how did you manage?'

'People were kind. You'd be surprised. We managed. And then the older kids moved out looking for jobs and the two younger ones and I moved into a caravan. We coped. You always cope.'

Don't you ever! Kathleen mused, sprawled on a settee on the restaurant veranda.

She felt awkward perched up on this ridge, as awkward as she had felt on the ridge at Lengakiki, her son an almost stranger in a stranger's arms in the too thin-walled room next to her own. Years of living informed her that they, too, were strangers with each other despite the arms, the nearness of flesh, the insistence of mouths. But there were communal moments for the three of them during the busying for lunch, bemoaning the rarity of guests, and on occasional night-times watching Nina Waterman sashay between cash register and tables, her splendidly rounded hips sustaining and embroidering rhythms pumped out by the stereo system. Such sensual confidence blinded her mind. *I was never like you, Nina*, she admitted, watching the bend and sway of body—but

never lubricious! nothing gross!—always re-
taining a hint of stimulating reserve as she sang
in early arrivals.

The two of them didn't want her to do
too much. They kept telling her this. She was
there to rest. They took dishes from her hand,
tea towels, serving spoons, vegetable knives.

'Take it easy, Mum,' Brain urged. His big
kindly face creased with concern on her behalf.
'Go look at the views. I'll bring you a drink.
What'll it be? Campari? Brandy cruster? Blue
Sunday? That's my special, the house special,
hey? I'm becoming a cocktail buff.'

Beyond them both the stunning view to
the coast folding down into the purple greys of
a pleated evening and Billie Holiday breaking
her heart and voice-box over a gloomier
version of the cocktail. In the dining room Nina
was torturing arrangements of hibiscus and
allamanda.

'I think you want to knock this old girl
out,' Kathleen had accused.

A week had gone by. They wouldn't let
her drive. She had always hated driving, anyway, in Brisbane's blazing car-jammed streets.
On the only occasion she had borrowed Brain's
car during her last visit north, she had lost her
way on a tableland back road and tipped the
car into a culvert.

Now she felt trapped. Was it second-hand kindness?

They had stacked her bedroom with paperbacks but her eyes tired easily these days and within ten minutes of opening a book a bestial languor closed her lids and she lolled inelegantly between dozing and waking, gasping in air through the wooden louvres of her room.

More and more profoundly she understood the mortality sentence, a fact she had avoided confronting for a lifetime.

One week became two, became three. Her cockahoop plumage sagged, depressed by her own presence, by Nina's studiously attentive manners and by Brain's fits of glumness.

What was happening to her house, she kept wondering aloud.

'When that compensation comes,' she informed her son, 'I'll be able to buy a small flat somewhere. I won't be such a nuisance.'

It could be years, Brain forbore telling her, for a government department to move its sluggish fingers towards writing a cheque; could be years before his mother found that suitable apartment.

He gritted his teeth at the thought of those longueurs. In the rough-hewn way of children he loved her, but he didn't want to live with her. No one, he told himself over and over, wanted to live with their parents on into the children's middle and later age while the parents struggled back into a drooling dotage. Anyway, he imagined chauvinistically, shouldn't a daughter?

He rang Sham.

'Don't ask me,' she said nastily and finally. 'We gave it a couple of months some years back. To be honest she was minding Bridgie for us part of the time. It just wouldn't work out. Not with Bridgie, anyway. She's at her most difficult. Sullen. Disobedient. Boys. God knows what else.'

'I thought Bridgie and mother got on. I thought they were buddies.'

'Well, that's their story. I know otherwise. Anyway, I've done my bit, Brain. It's up to you. Sometimes, I feel like getting a divorce from Bridgie, frankly.'

Frankly, Brain wanted to say, remembering the urgings and hormonal shovings of adolescence, you should. It was time. Time for Bridgie.

Instead he asked, 'Can't your bloody husband do anything about speeding up the compo payout, for God's sake?' and slammed the receiver down.

The landscape outside was saturated in

blue beneath the unrelenting heat and damp and windlessness which resolved every leaf along the restaurant veranda into a glittering plastic version of itself. For a moment he felt he was walking a tightrope of leaves. Through the open doorway he could see Nina looping bougainvillea fronds along overhead supports. His mother was lying in the bamboo recliner farther along, a book dropped from hands to lap, her glasses slipped from bridge of nose to tip. Elegant repetition. Briefly he wondered about Bimbo and Chaps, who were still chasing notions of jobs and ideas of accreditation in lost courses and causes in Brisbane. Really, mother would slot into one of their sporadic forays into communal living better than here. Her oddities were increasing with age, her indifference to convention running counter to the refinements and pretentiousness of her children's lifestyles. Would Bimbo and Chaps have a solution? Would they even bother considering the idea? Should he invite them up to help out? The sight of Nina meticulous with tendrils and plant tie made him scuttle that notion at the moment of launching. Childless, she had a distanced and almost icy irony with post-adolescents, treating them as if they were some recent archaeological find. She would listen and nod and comment and nod in a process of seduction—*I'm hanging on your every word!*—that burst in their faces as she delivered a pithy coup de grâce in the gentlest of voices, her lovely eyes warm with sympathy and concern.

Oh Nina! He had rocked with amusement on first observing her technique. Now?

'Oh shit!' he cried aloud, shocking his landscape with figures. 'Oh shit shit shit!'

It was all too much.

It had happened again.

Kathleen in the lounger at the southern end of the veranda woke from her half-sleep to the awareness of a warm puddling beneath her. She shoved an investigating paw down. Pants, shirt-tail and the water-resistant plastic cushions

were soaked with urine. Guiltily she eased herself out of the settee, glancing quickly at the
dining-room doors to see if Brain or Nina were
likely to come out, aware of voices arguing in
the kitchen. Confused and soggy and snivelling,
she gave the cushions a shake onto the veranda
boards thanking God that in that temperature
the stains would dry in minutes and slopped
down the stairs to take a side path to her bedroom in the cottage. She was trembling with
the humiliation of it. *Daisy, did it ever happen to
you? Did it?* Safe inside she dragged off the wet
clothes and changed. But when she was putting
the soiled garments to soak in the laundry tub,
Nina came in with a pile of luncheon cloths
ready for washing. Kathleen ran the taps vigorously, beating the detergent into a lather of
concealment. 'A little accident,' she said. There
was a compulsion to admit.

Nina smiled her archaic smile, lips curved
into a sprightly crescent. 'Darling, don't worry.
So long as you haven't done it in the presiden-
tial suite at the Casino. Still, on reflection, they
could do with that. I hear it's Japanese owned
now so perhaps we should say the imperial
suite.'

Kathleen heard herself gabble apologies,
her face blotched with embarrassment. 'If you
could just lend me a cloth I'll wipe off the
lounger.'

'Been there done that!' Nina said brightly.
Oh bitch!

'It's age,' her aged Brisbane doctor had
explained the first time it had happened. 'Your
sphincter muscles are getting tired. They're losing elasticity.'

'But it was on a bus. A long-distance bus.
They wouldn't turn the radio off.'

The doctor smiled. 'What a critic!' he said
admiringly. 'Now what I recommend . . .'

Brain ran her down to the local doctor for
a renewal of various scripts. He had waited
in the car, mulling over, in that sweatbox,
thoughts of retirement homes and villages, those
profiteering death camps with advertisements
of smiling well-groomed gents piloting blue-
rinsed freshly coiffured wives with such attentive hands they might still be in love. He wanted
to spew. Beyond those idly sauntering couples
seen through breeze-filled windows (*tease the
curtain a little, buster!*), there were always rolling
greens of mini golf courses, croquet lawns, the
impossibly blue waters of a micro pool (the body
corporate fees were tremendous) and the high-
netted perimeters of a half tennis court (could
the poor buggers actually play?), from whose
delights the wallet's ear might catch the sound
of inaccurately struck balls. Ah Christ!

He couldn't do that to Kathleen.

Or could he?

Wouldn't it, in the long run, he tried lying to himself, be better for everyone but mainly for her?

I have always wondered, she had said to Daisy, *why the power of the fist has always laid down moral and aesthetic codes, to say nothing of the rules for everyday living.* (I'll beat dat ole sin outa you!)

My, Daisy had said, *we are all high and intellectual today, aren't we? Remember you're talking to a beat-ee!*

They had been sitting in the Botanic Gardens, their old legs tottered to a stop by one of the embankment seats overlooking the river. Two hundred yards away an elderly man was being mugged by three youths in windcheaters. *It's the boys*, Daisy had said. *The chaps. They assume muscle power means brain power, poor loves, and whether it does or not they make the rules.* She had begun humming. *Ferally, ferally, shall I live now, under the dole cheque that hangs from the bough.* Kathleen started to giggle. *I'm a happy burden*, Daisy said.

But not to be a burden was what Kathleen wanted.

Drop me, she had ordered Brain a few days later, *at the airport*. And then there had been that *you don't have to go* nonsense that drove her mad and went on for at least two limp minutes — five minutes being a very long time — and Brain had agreed while she explained that she wanted to see if the highway had gone through her living room yet.

Will you be okay, then? he had asked in the terminal, his face concerned and too overtly relieved at the same time. She looked so small. *Will you? Will you be staying with Sham if anything goes wrong with the house?*

God forbid! she had said and they giggled guiltily together in the old way that had always made motherhood the very best thing.

'I'll let you know as soon as I get in,' she said firmly. 'I'll ring, dear.'

He feared what his sister might be planning, wasn't brave enough to face up to it, couldn't bear to have the ball, this grandma ball, bounce back into his court.

'Don't wait,' she said. 'I have to pee. Urgently.'

'Well, you know what gate then?' He checked her boarding pass and watched her head for Ladies. Her luggage had already been checked in.

'Okay Mum,' he said, running after her.

'Okay. If you're sure. We've got a big dinner party coming tonight. I'd better get back.'

But he waited until she returned from the washroom and saw her through the security gate into the passenger lounge.

'Hey!' he called after her. 'Hey! Take care.'

The cab dropped her outside the house. It looked the same. It looked different. Perhaps fear, that emotional spousing of her and home, was reaching an apex of rejection. On either side.

The veranda stretched its shade above the steps. Creepers choking uprights and coiling about finials dripped flowers onto a lawn over-grown from her absence and filled with weeds. Yet hollowness fell from the air.

To her probing key the front door creaked open on a shocking emptiness of disturbed and resettled dust. She pressed a light switch but nothing happened, and fumbling her way down the shadowy hall she felt for other switches, each of which was snuffed.

Sunlight washed through the breakfast room windows at the back of the house. It streamed over a void. Total. Tables, chairs, buffet had left only footprints on the linoleum. In the kitchen the space where the refrigerator had stood gaped its grimy outline. The stove had been wrenched from its cupboard fittings like an old tooth. Along the skirting board a cockroach moved disconsolately.

Shock therapy.

'God,' Kathleen breathed. She could have been praying. 'God God God.'

Dumping her bag on the floor and obliterating the cockroach, she went to her bedroom. Empty. The dining room. Empty. The living room. No cane loungers, leather easy chairs. No paraphernalia from the Pacific, its crystal blue now filled with the threat of storm. No television, mantel radio, clock. The telephone squatted on the floor, dead.

Room after room, empty. No beds, tables, chairs, pictures, mirrors, ornaments. Her mind played with the idea of crypts, of tombs. The built-in wardrobes were cleaned out except for two clothes hangers in one, huddling for comfort.

She wanted to cry but resentment was too strong to permit the slightest drip of moisture from her appalled eyes. Returning to the kitchen where not even a cup remained, curious, she turned on the tap over the sink but by the time her cupping hand reached beneath, the rusty water had dribbled into silence. It was as she stared hopelessly through the window at Brutus's kennel, desolate beneath the poinciana trees at the bottom of the yard, that she heard the slamming of a car door out front and the stiletto sharp heels of someone full of business as they ran up the front steps and down the emptied hall. Shamrock's little pointed chin thrust into dusty sunlight.

They stared at each other in the emptied kitchen, mother, daughter. Kathleen subsided gracelessly and deliberately to the floor.

'I can explain,' Shamrock proclaimed, in a voice heightened by the need for self-justification. She wore an ingratiating smile. 'Mother, do get up.'

'There's nowhere else to sit.'

'Oh Mother,' Shamrock said, full of her own outraged protest, 'Len and I . . .' She veered away and began on another tack. 'You can't possibly cope here. You know you can't. Len did it for the best. We were thinking of you. Truly. In any case the Department of Main Roads will be moving in any day.' She tried a girlish giggle. 'We had to beat those bulldozers, hadn't we?'

Kathleen refused to play descant to that insincere mirth. She thrust her legs out in an ungainly way. 'Had we?'

'Oh Mother! Now! Be realistic.'

Coda

Shamrock bent down and attempted to lift her mother. There was a moment of wrestling.

'Don't do that!' Kathleen said sharply. 'I am quite capable.' She heaved her body up, turned her back on her daughter and through the kitchen window saw neighbours on one side hanging out washing and on the other edging a car down the drive.

'I see no evidence of that. Not round me.' She could hear her words too high for utterance, it seemed, circling in uttermost space like windhovers. Her mouth opened but only gabble emerged.

Shamrock was shocked. 'Mother, please. Please don't be like that. I know what you're saying. But Len and I have booked you in to the most wonderful place. Look, we've been through all this. You know you can't manage.'

'I manage very well.'

'Oh you don't. You know you don't. You'll love the place we're taking you to. Really. You weren't meant, oh I know it's a shock, to come here and see all this. My bloody car broke down and by the time the service man came it was too late to reach you at the airport. Please, Mother, it's for the best. We've found this wonderful place.'

'What wonderful place?'

'Let's show you.'

Her daughter was insisting, persistent as always.

'You've taken all the chairs,' Kathleen heard herself complain, voice querulous and thin. 'There's nowhere to sit.'

'Come on. Come on out to the car.' Shamrock's not-so-gentle hand began steering her mother towards the front veranda.

'Don't touch me,' Kathleen said bitterly. 'What wonderful place?'

She planted herself on the veranda steps in the dead weight of her own resentment and looked up at Shamrock's self-seeking face, the ungenerous mouth, the too quick, too perceptive eyes.

'A retirement — no, don't be like that — a retirement village. Listen. Will you just listen! You have your own flat and you can eat in the communal dining room or not, just as you like. You can cook for yourself if you want. They'll even bring meals to your room. It's really very up to the minute.'

Kathleen spat out her comment. 'Flat, care, coffin. It's a money-grubbing racket. Meals brought to your room! At what cost, I wonder. Communal dining. Oh God Almighty, Sham I like to choose the faces that confront me over the cereal. For heaven's sake, what have you done?'

'Please, please, don't be like this.' Shamrock eased her mother up again and was attempting to direct her to the car.

'Where are all my clothes, my books?'

'They're packed and waiting for you.'

'Where?'

'At Passing Downs.'

'*Where?*'

Shamrock blushed.

'*Passing Downs?*' Kathleen was savage with emphasis. 'Oh my God! And the furniture? Where's the furniture?'

'Do get into the car, Mother. I'm afraid we've sold that.'

'Sold? How on earth did you manage that? And the house? What about my house?'

'It's listed for sale. Well, actually, it's been sold already to the Department of Main Roads.'

Kathleen heard hoarse shouts struggle from her throat that was already clotted with years of resentment.

'You can't do that. Legally you can't do that.'

Shamrock opened the car door, forcing her mother into the passenger seat, and raced furiously around to slam her own way in. The two women sat staring straight before them along the baking road. At last Shamrock dredged up words.

'Don't you remember? Oh Mother, don't you remember anything? You gave Len power of attorney. Can't you recall signing those papers he brought out just before you went north to stay with Brain? Please Mother, try to remember. You really did sign them when you heard what the DMR was about to do.'

'Oh God.' Kathleen wept hopelessly. Her eyes and nose streamed and she wiped carelessly at her melting face with the sleeve of her worn cotton jacket. 'Oh God. I don't want to leave. I don't want to.'

'You've got no choice, Mum.'

'Don't Mum me, Shamrock. You've got the empathy of a piranha. And what about Brutus? How will Brutus fit in with this elegant retirement privateer?' She began wrestling the car door open and stepped groggily onto the kerb.

'Look Mother, get back in the car will you? For God's sake sit down at least.'

'I don't want to sit. I want you to drive me to the kennels to pick up Brutus.'

Her daughter's lips snapped shut briefly on resentment, impatience, and now the blood pressure of rage. She clutched the steering wheel, fighting for control.

'Just get in the car.'

'Where's Brutus?'

Jaw clamped in its pretty stubborn lines,

tongue tensing on the horrible confession she
would have to make, Shamrock flung open the
car door once more and stalked her fury round
the car.

'There,' she said, half shoving her mother
back into the Mercedes. She locked the door.
'Now.' Neighbours in the next house had paused
in their gardening and were moving closer to
listen. One of them waved. Ignoring this,
Shamrock stomped back to the driving seat and
started the motor before her mother could make
further desperate moves. The air conditioner
worked busily at filtering Quelques Fleurs and
the more pungent stench of selfishness and the
car rapidly left Ascot behind.

'I said where's Brutus?'

'Len had him put down.' The young
woman had decided on brutality in the maze of
traffic.

'What?'

'There was nothing else for it.' She snapped
on the car radio to a burst of metal rock. Her
mother leaned over and snapped it off.

'What do you mean nothing else? Oh God
you obnoxious rotten pair. Oh Christ! How
could you do this?' Kathleen turned her dis-
traught face to observe her daughter's frozen
profile and looked hard and long. 'You know,'
she said, 'you're becoming quite ugly.'

The dried-out heart dried out the eyes. There was nothing left to shed, neither tears nor hurt, only shock at betrayal so basic and so swift and unexpected, it was as if the body were stunned by electrodes. She would be excised from the world's grief. In this shabby, beautiful existence coincidences were the concomitants of chaos and she recalled with satisfaction Bridgie's story of Len and the secretary. Sham had allowed the wrong animal to be put down, she thought, and began to giggle at the admitted irony.

Muted, she allowed herself to be taken. The car was an enclosed loony bin with its dark tinted windows racing along the blistered tarmac of Brisbane streets, over bubbling asphalt transcriptions of hell pavements to some outer bayside suburb and the horror of gardened-to-death villas in their box-like, coffin-like rows. In the shade of newly planted shrubberies she would and did discover when they arrived, various old bodies slumped on plastic chairs or staggering on walking frames. There was no conversation. There was a mummified indifference, each remnant-being concerned solely with its own privations, which it was desperate to prolong, and the suffering inflicted by corporately conceived comfort.

The silent scream.

In a foyer related more to a hotel chain than a caring system, a pretence of efficiency came with starched uniform and impeccable makeup.

'They'll look after you here, Mum. You'll be right here. Len has shares in the place.'

What a foolish child she had bred, Kathleen decided, hearing those idiot Judas words.

With elaborate modulation, she said to the receptionist, alert over a poised ballpoint and admission form, 'I have no intention of staying in this place.'

'Come now, Mrs Hackendorf,' the receptionist said, all smiles and warmth, 'just let us show you to your room. I'm sure when you see it you'll change your mind.'

'You're wearing too much mascara. No.'

'Really, Mrs Hackendorf!' The receptionist was used to dealing with addle-heads.

'But Mother,' Shamrock hissed, dutiful daughter, 'your clothes, everything, they're all set up here.'

'Do you take dogs?' Kathleen asked, leaning towards the receptionist.

'No pets, I'm afraid.'

'Why are you afraid? By the way, you look like a tart.' She paused and winked at the receptionist. 'Some of my best friends are . . .'

'Mother!'

The receptionist rolled her eyes at the ceiling and produced a key that she handed to Shamrock. 'Suite 2 down this corridor, first turning to the left . . . I'll be with you in a moment.' She pressed a buzzer. 'Sister,' she called into the intercom. 'Sister. We have a new guest.'

Kathleen's lead-plugged feet trailed the white walls behind her daughter, remembering all those times when, the position reversed, Shamrock had whinged and dragged at museum visits, art gallery tours, dental procedures. 'Acheron Lodge,' she kept muttering. 'Styx Villas. Avernal Shades.'

'Please,' Shamrock kept pleading. 'Please.'

'What room?' her mother asked. 'Charnel number 5?'

'Oh my God, not funny!' Shamrock cried, thrusting the key in a lock and flinging open a door.

The room was microscopic. At one end an idea of a kitchenette. At the other a door opened on to a lavatory and shower. There were griprails for the elderly, a discretion of beige paint and ash-coloured carpet, the colour of tears, two plastic chairs beside a plastic table, a narrow bed. Did she imagine the beating of dark wings?

'When you get a few of your things in, Mum,' Shamrock whispered, 'it will be a lot better.'

'But you've sold all my things. And WHY' —she suddenly raised her voice and began to shout—'ARE YOU WHISPERING?'

Shamrock bit her lip.

A nurse appeared, a walloper of professional cheer. A matron joined them. They made quite a crowd in the tiny room. The smiles stiffened as Kathleen said, 'It's like that Groucho Marx film, *A Night at the Opera*. If I hadn't known Shamrock I'd never have got this room.'

The matron nodded and nodded. She prided herself on her understanding of these difficult moments. Her smile became ossified. 'Well,' she asked, her face assuming that spurious but rigid tolerance of a cabinet minister confronted by genuine grievance, 'and what do you think of this, then? Quite a view, isn't it?' Even as they stared through glass across the four-foot wide balcony at the green lawns, they saw an elderly man topple sideways from his wheelchair.

'I think,' Kathleen stated clearly but unemphatically, 'it's fucking awful.'

Corpsed.

On her unresisting bed Kathleen worked at the edges of sleep. She mourned Brutus, muddling him with Daisy from whom she had inherited him. *Never mind, Daise*, she said aloud in the coffin room of Passing Downs. *He's better off*.

When Daisy had failed to show that time, so long ago now, she had rung the number kept for emergencies. The neighbour told her Daisy was dead. In that choking noise-filled silence the man's voice kept coming through with questions. *Her things? Her dog? She hasn't any things*, she had told him. *Nothing that matters*. All the same she had taken a train down the bay and trudged up to the Shorncliffe headland, seeing the flat waters as Daisy must have seen them, day after day. It was true. Nothing. The cheap bits of crockery, the cut-out pictures from magazines tacked to the wall, the exhausted over-laundered bedding became now an ironic metaphor of the house she had just been wrenched from.

Brutus was a large elderly dog of untrackable ancestry and a clumsy gentle temper. All he owned was a collar and a half-empty packet of dog food.

'I'll take him,' she said to the neighbour.

The neighbour ran them both back to town, Brutus lying miserably in the tray of the van. Kathleen held back her tears until her front door closed and then she managed to wipe off the last of her grieving on Brutus's rough old coat. Within a week he had settled in, had the run of the house and slept on the front veranda. He now owned a new food bowl and a kennel which he rarely entered, but in the way of dogs he quickly re-established his loyalties, wagging as they watched television together, grunting, snoring, making appalling and uninhibited smells and putting up an elderly paw to be shaken. *He thinks I'm Daisy*, Kathleen admitted. *We smell the same. Both old.*

So long, Brutus, she said in the sleepless dark and fumbled for a lamp switch. There was none. Easing herself out of bed she went to the bathroom and groped through her toilet bag for a pill, a blinder, a knockout drop.

Ah!

She stayed two nights, caused havoc at mealtimes by insisting on smoking, refused to join in the parlour games of scrabble or punt balls through croquet hoops on the lawn, packed an overnight bag and left on the morning of the third day.

The taxi dropped her at the shell of her house and she told the driver to wait while she went inside. Her own pain had settled along with the dust on window ledges and the sun-scoured strips of floor. Shamrock had removed the last of the curtains. Even the mud-scraper mat was gone. No one had mentioned the results of the sale which, she imagined as she looked about, could not have amounted to much. The minister for transports must have done a private deal with the Department of Main Roads. Where was her money?

She went back to the taxi, her heart pumping faster with anger, and asked to be driven to the city. Her lawyer had rooms above a bookstore in Alice Street and her irruption was a compounded flurry of bile and absent-mindedness that overcame her suddenly as she sat in the waiting room. Her bladder was making demands. Why was she there? She was used to meeting Daisy near the washrooms in Adelaide Street.

'The lavatory?' she managed to ask the girl behind the desk, who stared at this crazy bag lady in distaste.

'It's for staff only,' she said primly. (*Go wet yourself!*)

'Tell me,' Kathleen heard this old girl shout, 'or I'll piss the floor.'

'Why, Kathleen,' exclaimed a tortoise head poked round the opened office door. 'After all this time! Show Mrs Hackendorf the conveniences, dear, and then bring us two coffees.'

To her horror Kathleen found herself weeping, weeping as she rinsed her hands in the basin, weeping as she straightened her dowdy hat and came back into the outer office. Behind her the cistern flushed uncontrollably. The irritated receptionist went off with little mutterings to flick faulty levers. But Kathleen had remembered now why she had come, and even the luke-warm coffee and the client-geared easy chair failed to reassure her.

The tortoise was telling her that the house had indeed been sold to a government department. (A screwed hanky dabbed at fury.) She had been foolish to sign away power of attorney. As far as he could see — and there was much paper shifting and pen fiddling — it was a private arrangement between her son-in-law and a state authority.

'I want the money.'

The solicitor smiled. 'We can send a letter of demand.' He smiled more widely. He loathed the minister, whose rudeness and self-complacency were of a glittering impregnability.

'If you could prove force, that you were unaware of what you were signing. These things are difficult. Were you aware?'

Kathleen could only shake her head. 'I can't remember.'

The solicitor leaned across his desk and pinned her with his eyes. 'You don't know any journalists, do you? They could whip this up. The papers would love to get hold of something like this.' Kathleen saw him momentarily licking his lips. '"State member renders mother-in-law homeless".' He tried a headline or two and Kathleen, drawn abruptly from resentment, found herself laughing.

'I like that.'

'Do you? Well, we can work on it. I must say that if the letter of demand brings no response, you can sue, but it's such a lengthy business. I strongly suggest you get in touch with your friendly neighbourhood press.' He smirked. 'By the way, where are you staying?'

She hesitated. He appeared sympathetic. She hoped he was that in a world she now saw as full of deceit. But the oily glister to his bald pate might be even more synthetic than the easy surface of his words. 'Oh,' she replied. 'Oh my daughter took me out to this terrible retirement village. Ghastly. I simply can't stay.'

'What's the name of the place?'

Caution rode her smile. 'Spent Forces. Twigdroppers. I really can't remember. I've no intention of going back.'

'But Mrs Hackendorf—Kathleen—probably that is where the money went. On buying you a place there. A villa, I think they call them. Remember, I handled only the actual sale of your house in the most minimal way. Your son-in-law told me nothing. It was the barest formality—sighting signatures and so on. Of course that's what happened! A unit, villa, whatever. If that's the case it would be even harder to get your money back. Most of those places have very tight fine print. It's all their way. Frankly, I think that taking your son-in-law to court as well as the retirement village, to say nothing, my dear, of a government authority, would be expensive and useless. You'd lose and you would be worse off than you are now. I'm sorry.'

'You're sorry!'

She walked slowly back to the Queen Street walking-place, a madhouse of tent-topped eateries and truant schoolkids rampaging past shop fronts. She was buffeted by racing hoons on roller blades and shoving teenagers, rendered invisible to them by her very age. Someone snatched at her overnight bag, dragging her off her feet while she clung and clung, the paving stripping skin from knuckles and elbows. A cluster of other ancients had gathered then and she was being helped up, her bag with its broken strap still at her feet. A woman—Daisy?—shoved it into her shaking hand.

'Bloody louts,' the old geezer with the paunch commented. His anxious sun-battered face looked hard at her. 'You've hurt your arm, lady. It's these damn pupil-free days they're all having. And no bloody police when you want them. You all right, then?'

Her noddle see-sawed, but not with agreement—in a kind of frenzied waggle she couldn't control. On the grubby shirt-front close to her eyes there were friendly food stains, the stigmata of decline and its ultimate indifference; a sheen of sweat greased the wrinkled neck above. Babble words about her seemed to clatter with concern.

'A cab,' she mumbled. 'I need a cab.'

'Come on, then, love, I'll get you there. Just a bit of a way down here on your left.' The little knot of curious watchers loosened, untied and drifted away. 'Hang on to me, missus, and I'll take you all right. Bloody louts. There ought to be a law.'

This is nice, Kathleen thought, this warmth of strangers. Support from that beefy slab of arm helped her forget the needle-sting

of her torn elbow while he reined in his strides
to equate with her own stumbling feet.

'There you go.'

Calvary over. The cab door opened and
she felt arms lever her onto a seat where, dazed,
she sat mindless of destinations.

Where?

Stranger comfort had vanished and the
driver was impatiently repeating his question,
head half-turned, eyes rolling in mock despair
at this stupid biddy. 'I said where to, lady.'

'Airport,' she said. The impulse that had
lain there all day awaiting her recognition was
grabbed with a tired delight, a sense of solution.

'Domestic or international?'

Was there irony? This crumpled old bat
was spattered with blood, her bag strap dangled
torn, her hat sat cock-eyed.

'Domestic,' she whispered.

He turned the cab radio up full onto some
talentless screamer and Brisbane laid out its
steaming spaces for them, flattened under its
own muggy effusions as they drove too fast
through the headache that was threatening to
split her skull open.

Limbo.

This is the magic hall of mirrors. Just stand in front of the glass displaying your number and boy, are you ever in for a surprise!

There goes Ronald on a windjammer, beating before the Trades, looking for landfalls that ultimately he does not want. Or if he glides into an unencumbered harbour, he soon tires, sets sail (gifts of breadfruit, papayas heaped on the deck, chanting and weeping natives watching his departure from the shoreline growing smaller and smaller as his ship swings with the tides) and, cursed (a blast of trumpets!) like Vanderdecken, is doomed to never-ending arrivals and embarkations.

Watching that wind-tousled young man

at the tiller, he can only smile. He's never thought far beyond weighing anchor.

Like me, Brain supposes, seeing a distorted self screeching out numbers on the floor of Wall Street stock exchange, waving at the guys on the rostrum, begging to buy, sell, make it this time. He has always dreamed of millions, the exquisiteness of zeros. But hey, wait a minute! Wait a minute, bud! He's not dabbling in shares. He's singing, for Chrissake! The guy's letting them have it, full voice. He can see his mouth making the sound hit the front of his palate, even the strainings of his diaphragm. But what are the words? What are the goddam words? Not Tosti, not shanty, not *Lied*. He's urging these bulls and bears of the pit to take a pair of sparkling eyes.

Sister Shamrock is delighted to observe herself hosting a dinner party for fifty (who has a table *that* large!) power-brokers, heads of state, paper millionaires. It's a setting of crystal, starched napery, and deliciously presented food. But my God, what's this? The lobster stinks! The chilled wine's like vinegar and she's sure that at the other end of the table Len has his hand up that woman's skirt.

My turn, Kathleen says impatiently to the guide. *My turn*. He leads her over to the glass and that's her number all right, but when she looks in the mirror it is milky, purblind, the surface a pallid emulsion that washes sluggishly within the frame. *What's this then?* she asks the guide, who is shuffling his feet. *Don't I get a look?*

 That's it, lady, the guide says.

She must have dozed, for something jerked her back to the present in the high tide of summer scalding the paving and the gloss-painted bench where she sat. She groped for her overnight bag. It was still there, packed with a change of clothing, her pills, some basic toilet items and tissues. To mop up—what? What was it? Tears? She couldn't recall what it was she should be upset about. Lear, forget it, you selfish mug!

Only a male would have mewled about the front doors of castles that didn't want him, desperate for the four-minute egg, the lightly buttered toast.

She began walking slowly along the mall a little way to the sea end and plumped herself down in the shade of the overhead gallery restaurant. Water bubbled, palms flapped despairing signals over the shoppers and the grubby glitz of shop fronts. She remembered her suitcase taken south three days ago, forgotten as she left the airport, which could still be circling endlessly on the Brisbane carousel. Someone might snatch it, she speculated uninterestedly. She didn't really care. She hoped it would be a disappointed transvestite confronted by four sets of practical underwear, a cotton twinset and assorted cheap slacks and shirts that bore her indelible post-middle-aged shape. *Me bum!* she thought. *He'll hate me bum.*

Now she could see Daisy coming slowly up the mall, trudging in the terrible heat, her hat dragged low so the brim sheltered her face. Daisy was slowing up too, poor old girl, she couldn't help noticing. Soon, she told herself, she would take the ferry and cross over to the island unlike those other islands that were locked, seed floaters, into her past, across which the shadows growing shadowier of old island hands moved: Ronald, the assistant secretary who had once . . ., the manager of the Joy Biscuit Company. Perhaps Daisy would come with her. She would miss their weekly meetings. And then she realised it wasn't Daisy at all, Daisy in Brisbane, herself here, and she drowsed for a moment but was snapped awake by words cutting the air about her, swooping bird-like as she blinked into the afternoon glare. She forced herself up and began walking diagonally to another tea room in one of the arcades.

A short dumpy woman with a moustache was sitting humbly at one of the tables, edged so close to the brink of her chair it appeared she wanted to make no more impression, occupy no more space, than was humanly necessary. Kathleen's eyes met those of the waiting woman and she smiled, receiving in return the most timorous, the most tentative, of responses under that emphatic moustache. Oh God! Kathleen thought. Oh God! The eyes of the stranger had that wondering pained look of innocent blue that for a life-time had been fearful of catching the appraising stare, the smirk, the noisy glee of kids. She had been sniggered at too long. Even her clothes were steeped with despair.

Kathleen smiled again, despising her self-conscious charity; but loneliness created a mist around this discard. 'Lovely day,' Kathleen said.

'Lovely day.' She moved past and away, ah, the shame of it, but the woman with the moustache was suddenly walking beside her, timid, frightened to intrude.

'Hallo, Daisy,' Kathleen said.

'I'm not Daisy.'

Kathleen blinked. Heat dazzle overcame her. 'Aren't you?' she said vaguely. 'I'm sorry. I thought . . . I get muddled these days. Brisbane. An old friend I used to meet. I was just going for a cup of tea.'

The hopefulness on the face under the hat brim defied her indifference, compounded error. They walked back to the tea room together.

This was pleasant. Sitting. Free. Sipping. Sitting. She could pretend it was Daisy. Free now to pretend anything at all.

Tourists ambled by in their crease-proof, stinkingly hot tropic gear. The air-conditioning in the little cafe hummed like the sea and she forgot entirely the ugly retirement home, the bulldozers flattening a highway through the living room of the house at Ascot, smashing the bric-à-brac memories of decades there and the ghost relics of those months in the islands.

'We could be friends,' the old girl with the mo was suggesting, another moustache of cappuccino stuck to the one already there.

Kathleen had to laugh. 'Why not?' she

agreed. 'I'm off to the island soon.' She had only the vaguest notions of what she would do next. It was safe to think in clichés. They protected, gave succour. There was some money, she remembered, straining for practicality, that she didn't really care about. Not a lot. A public service pension that drizzled brief fortnightly puddles of support into her bank account like a rusty tap. She had a few hundred in savings. Who cared? Who damn well cared?

'Who cares?' she said to the moustache, which quivered away from her sharp demand. She didn't. She had spent—well—half a lifetime worrying about the fortunes of her children, who now proved myopic and deaf about hers. And who cared about that? Not gutsy Kathleen who heard herself say to this shaken old bod in the chair opposite, 'It's time to go feral. Tribes of feral grandmothers holed up in the hills, just imagine it, refusing to take on those time-honoured mindings and moppings up after the little ones while the big ones jaunt into the distance.' The moustache quivered along an amused but frightened lip. 'Always grandmothers,' she was shouting now. 'They never put the hard word to mind on grandpops. Old men. Because they're afraid they'll shove their fingers up the kids' bums or worse. Isn't that so?' she demanded, leaning forward to the grinning but alarmed face across the cups. 'Still,' she ranted, ignoring the waitress's tap on the shoulder, 'still . . .' She stopped, bemused, forgetting what it was she had intended to say.

'You're getting loud,' the moustache whispered.

'Oh Daisy,' Kathleen asked, 'why in heaven are you wearing that moustache?'

She couldn't understand when the old girl burst into tears.

She met the moustache head on, decided to delight in it and those blameless, baffled eyes that gazed out above trumped-up questions to strangers about bus times or whereabouts, driven by isolation and the need to speak to someone, anyone, to prove she was human, capable of communion, of receiving the ultimate wafer host of words.

The sadness of it.

Kathleen offered her best, her sweetest smile, touched by the other woman's dilemma in the essential ugliness of a Hollywood world and said, 'My daughter, my son and the minister for transports have no idea at all how to smile,' and wondered as the puzzlement on her listener's face rose and bubbled and drained away as if even those words held some further jibe inexplicable for the moment.

She paid for the tea and wandered out

again along the mall, heading east with the curve of the river, pausing now and then to stare in a shop window or look at family groups clustered about the fast-food stalls. She turned around, waiting for Daisy, expecting her to catch up. 'Daisy?' she called. 'Hey, Daisy!' But there was no one behind her now. No one. Had she imagined that other?

Farther on she thought she spied the moustache once more and she smiled widely and warmly and waved a hand. But the moustache retreated behind the bodies of other strollers and Kathleen forgot almost at once. 'Trust Daisy to be late!' she muttered, irritable. 'Trust her!' The island, she decided giving her bag a little shake. She must reach the island. Magnetic. It had meant, or started, something years and years ago. She was heading for the source. Magnetic. Though smiles weren't, that very word determined the direction of her hot and aching feet towards the ferry terminals.

Despite the searing lick of the sun when she left the shelter of the awnings, her world appeared as nothing more than a celestial blue blister inside which lumbered a rocking ultramarine water, across which she would soon be bobbing.

Scraps of poetry took possession, something scribbled decades back in the primacy of arrival there: *thoughts pointed to the pole-star of the mind, move into light*—it was light, wasn't it?—*from outer dark like ships unhurried.* 'Oh yes,' she said aloud. 'Oh yes oh yes oh yes.' There was more if it would come, if those creeping words could reach and grope upwards to this fuzzy brain. '*Tacking towards that centre, foam-defined,*' she declaimed to the mid-afternoon street.

Her feet, limping along iambics and tro-chees, had reached the entrance to the ferry building before she knew it. Nothing like a bit of verse to take the mind off! Fragments of phrase, shreds of metaphor took her through to the ticket office and the narrow catwalk to the landing, along which passengers were already moving, pressing down the gangway and tak-ing their seats on the ferry.

'Ah, the *Fort Caribee*!' Kathleen said to the deckhand, who hadn't a clue.

She swung her bag lightly, forgetting everything, stepping renewed into the boat and sitting up front behind the glittering windows now streaked with spray as the ferry took the tides of the crossing. Not a cloud anywhere. Only this preserving, baking, astringent blue.

There was more poetry if she could simply catch hold of it. More. *Upon my brow*, she strug-gled to remember, *winds patterned*—was it patterned?—*with palmetto find the calms beyond great longing*. Ah, there! The calms! She was scrabbling and rooting about for words in that old handbag of her years. *Young, I magnify*— that was it, *magnify!*—*the island moving in across the prow!*

Young!

'God!' she said aloud to the world at large, to anyone who would listen. 'What a marvellous day!'